At Whispering Pine Lodge

Lawrence J. Leslie

AT WHISPERING PINE LODGE

BY LAWRENCE J. LESLIE

1919

CONTENTS

CHAPTER

I.   THE HALT ON THE ADIRONDACK CARRY
II.   GRIPPED BY A GIANT'S UNSEEN HANDS
III.   OBED GRIMES BOBS UP
IV.   BANDY-LEGS SUSPECTS
V.   PACKING OVER THE "CARRY"
VI.   THE LODGE OF MANY WONDERS
VII.   THE YOUNG MAGICIAN
VIII.   PRODUCTS OF THE FUR FARM
IX.   LAYING PLANS TO HELP OBED
X.   TRAPS FOR NIGHT PROWLERS
XI.   A TREE THAT BORE STRANGE FRUIT
XII.   THE TAPS ON THE CABIN WALL
XIII.   OBED LEARNS SOMETHING
XIV.   A BIG SURPRISE
XV.   STEVE'S DREAM COMES TRUE
XVI.   THE FUR FARMER'S TRIUMPH—CONCLUSION

THE OBLONG BOX.

CHAPTER I

THE HALT ON THE ADIRONDACK CABBY

"Where's Touch-and-Go Steve, fellows?"

"Why, Max, he slipped away with his little steel-jointed fishing-rod as soon as he heard you say we'd stop here over night. And I saw him picking some fat white grubs out of those old rotten stumps we passed at the time we rested, an hour back. Huh! just like Slippery Steve to get out of the hard work we've going to have cutting enough brush for making our shanty shelter tonight; seeing that we didn't fetch our bully old tent along this trip. He's a nice one, I should say."

"N-n-never you m-m-mind about Steve, Bandy-legs. He t-t-told me he *knew* he c-c-could yank a m-m-mess of fine trout out of that c-c-creek, where it looked so s-s-shallow just back there. He's m-m-meaning to w-w-wade in, too, I reckon, and when you s-s-smell the fish c-c-cooking you'll be s-s-sorry you said what you did."

"Well, let's get a move on, and start that shanty. I chose this place partly on account of there being so much brush handy, you see."

"Sure you did, Max. It takes you to notice things that miss our eyes. Here, let me handle the hatchet, because you see I was such a truthful little shaver away back that my folks often regretted they hadn't named me George Washington."

"All I c-c-can say then, Bandy-legs, they b-b-builded wiser than they knew when they j-j-just let it g-g-go at regrets. A f-f-fine George Washington you'd m-m-make, I'm thinking."

The boy answering to the peculiar name of "Bandy-legs" laughed good-naturedly as he began to swing the sharp-edged hatchet, and cut down some of the required brush which, having camped many times before, he knew was suitable for their requirements.

Besides this sturdy young chap with the lower limbs that were a little bowed, and which fact had doubtless suggested such a nickname to his schoolmates, there were two others busily engaged in gathering the material to be used in affording them a rude, but effective shelter during the coming night.

The one whom they called Max seemed to be looked upon as a leader, for it is absolutely necessary that in every pack of boys some one takes the initiative. His whole name was Max Hastings, and on numberless occasions he had shown an aptitude for "doing things" when the occasion arose, that gained him the respect of his chums. For a complete record of these achievements the reader is referred to earlier volumes of this series, where between the covers will be found much interesting and instructive reading.

The third boy of the trio in sight was Toby Jucklin. While Toby was certainly agile enough when it came to acrobatic stunts, and such things as boys are fond of indulging in, his vocal cords often loved to play sad pranks with his manner of speech. As the reader has already discovered, Toby was fain to stutter in the most agonizing fashion. When one of these fits came upon him he would get red in the face, and show the greatest difficulty in framing certain words. Then all of a sudden, as though taking a grip on himself, Toby would stop short, draw in a long breath, give a sharp whistle, and strange to say, start talking as plainly as the next one.

In time perhaps he would conquer this weakness, which after all is only caused by nervousness, and a desire to rattle out words.

There was a fourth chum also, the Steve spoken of and who had slipped away with his new steel-jointed bait-rod, and a handful of fat grubs, as soon as he heard Max say they had gone far enough on their way. Steve, being one of those hasty lads who do a thing while many people would be only figuring it out, had long ago fallen heir to a number of suggestive nicknames, among others "Touch-and-Go Steve," and "Old Lightning."

These four lads were a long ways from their home town of Carson, nestled on the Evergreen River, and near which we have seen them in the earlier books of this series successfully carry out numerous of their undertakings.

In fact they were deep in the wildest part of the famous Adirondacks at the time we run across them on this particular occasion. There was not a town within many miles, nor for that matter a regular camp where summer guests were entertained. The difficulties to be encountered along this "carry" were so great that ordinary excursionists avoided it severely. Indeed, few fishermen ever invaded these solitudes, although there were undoubtedly many places where trout of generous size might be picked up.

All this would make it seem a bit queer that Max and his three chums should venture into this section of the wilderness without a guide along; so perhaps it might be wise to enter upon explanations while the opportunity is open.

Now these tried and true chums had had strange things happen to them before, but they were well agreed that their present undertaking far exceeded everything else that had ever come their way, at least so far as its being a romantic quest was concerned.

Everything combined to make it seem a page torn from one of those old-time fairy books they used to love to read when much younger, and more gullible. In the first place, it was a wonderful piece of luck that came their way, when the School Directors agreed, after the summer was half over, that the school buildings required considerable alterations in order to make them sanitary for the coming winter; and really a special providence that watches over the fortunes of boys and girls must have caused the carpenters and masons to go on a protracted strike, so that when this had been finally settled there was not nearly time enough left in which to complete the extensive repairs.

School had started, and gone along in a rough-and-ready fashion for some weeks; but everybody was "sore" about it. The builders complained that they could not accomplish half the work they should, because of the annoyance of having so many children trotting around, and bothering them. And the teachers were almost distracted on account of the constant pounding together with the presence of rough men, who broke in upon classes, and forced them to vacate certain rooms because they had to do something there.

And so along about the first of October the School Board wisely concluded that a vacation of some two weeks would do far less harm to the scholars than a continuation of these interruptions. Besides, the teachers on their part threatened to also strike unless relief came promptly.

Imagine the delight of such fellows as Max, Bandy-legs, Steve and Toby Jucklin, all of whom loved life in the open so much, when they got the chance to further indulge this propensity, especially at the most glorious time of the whole year, when the nut crop was coming on, the trees turning red and yellow from the magical touch of Jack Frost's cold fingers, with a tang in the air that made a fellow twice as hungry as he ever got in the hot old summer-time.

And then, as though Fate had determined to make this the most wonderful of periods in all their checkered careers, a thing happened that seemed just like one of those old but once much beloved fairy stories.

Perhaps, by listening to the workers exchanging comments as they gather the necessary brush, which later on would be fashioned into a shelter capable of shedding even a moderate amount of rain, we may be able to pick up enough general information to understand the nature of their mission up into the Adirondacks.

Bandy-legs was speaking at the time. He had a little fault in the way of often showing a disposition to look at the darker side of things; and doubtless being unusually tired, after a hard day's tramp, with such a heavy pack on his back, had something to do with his spirit of complaining on the present occasion.

"Well, all I can say, fellows," he remarked, as he carried an armful of the stuff he had been gathering to the spot where Max had already commenced to erect the sides of the squatty shelter by driving stakes into the ground, "is that I hope we haven't come all the way up here on a reg'lar fool's errand. It'd cost Mrs. Hopewell a pretty good sum, and be a real disappointment to her, if after all we didn't find that good-for-nothing nephew of hers, Roland Chase. Honest to goodness now, I'm a little inclined to believe he'll be leading us a wild-goose Chase, if you want my opinion."

"Oh! l-l-let up, c-c-can't you, Bandy-legs!" spluttered the indignant Toby, pausing for a minute to wipe the beads of perspiration from his brow, and regain his breath in the bargain. "You're g-g-getting to be a regular old g-g-granny, that's what, with all your d-d-dismal p-p-prophesies. Tell me, d-d-did we *ever* f-f-fail yet in anything we undertook? C-c-course we haven't. Right in the start we found all those b-b-bully p-p-pearls in those mussels we g-g-gathered in the Big Sunflower River, and laid away a n-n-nice n-n-nest-egg in bank for the crowd. Sure we'll f-f-find Roland Chase; we've just g-g-got to, that's all."

"All I want to say about it, boys," observed Max, "is that I admire the grit of the boy. They told us he was something of a dude, didn't they, and that his rich uncle was afraid he'd never amount to much anyhow; so what did he do but make a most *extraordinary* will; at least, everybody who's heard about that proviso says so. I heard Judge Perkins say though he guessed the old man knew boys better than most folks, and had taken a wise course to prove whether this Roland had any snap in him or not."

"Well, he was left just two thousand dollars cash down," said Bandy-legs, in a thoughtful manner, as though reviewing the singular circumstance, "and if at the end of two years he could show that he had doubled that amount, besides earning his own living, why he was to come into two-thirds of his uncle's fortune. Some of our Carson people who know folks over in Sagamore where the uncle lived tell whopping big stories about the size of that fortune. I heard one man say he reckoned it was as much as two hundred thousand dollars, in all."

"The funny part of it is," resumed Max, shaking his head in a way rather odd for him, "that immediately after Roland received his two thousand in cash he disappeared from the scene. That was almost two years ago; and from that day nobody in Sagamore has ever had a peep at him. The fact is he might almost be dead. Once his other aunt, Mrs. Hopewell, who lives now in Carson, had a few lines from Roland. He simply said he was alive and well, and that he had hopes of seeing her again one of these fine days."

"Yes, that's r-r-right," burst out Toby, in a disgusted tone, "but not a p-peep did he give about what he was d-d-doing, or if he meant to show up and c-c-claim his f-f-fine f-f-fortune. And all she could make out was that the p-p-postmark on the l-l-letter was Piedmont, N.Y., which on looking up we f-f-found was away up here in the h-h-heart of the old Adirondacks."

"Well," said Max, still working industriously away, "Mrs. Hopewell is getting very much concerned about Roland. Somehow she seemed to fancy the boy, though no one else thought he'd ever amount to anything, because he used to like to wander around in the woods all the while, or go fishing, instead of studying. But I guess those people hadn't ever been boys themselves; and all of us can appreciate this liking for the open that Roland showed."

"And so," pursued Bandy-legs after the fashion of a story-teller who had-reached a crisis in his tale, "she asked Max here if he wouldn't be willing to undertake a trip to the mountains with several of his good chums, meaning us, fellows, to try and locate the missing Roland, and bring back some encouraging news; for the good old soul is in great fear that the second year will soon be finished, and unless Roland is able to show four thousand dollars in cash, most of the estate will go to his older cousin, Frederick. Mrs. Hopewell dislikes this chap very much, because she says he is a bad man, who drinks, and gambles, and does all sorts of things old ladies detest. Well, we took her up in a jiffy as soon as we heard the glorious news about school being closed for two weeks; and as she foots all the bills, we're bound to have a jolly time of it, even if we don't run across Roland; and I think that is like looking for a needle in a haystack."

That was a pretty long speech for even Bandy-legs to make, and yet it covered considerable of the ground, and explained just how it came that Max and his three comrades chanced to be so far away from the home town.

The boys were just about to turn their attention once more to the work that had been undertaken when all of them suddenly stopped and listened.

"That was Steve yelling then, I reckon," snapped the owner of the bowed legs, "but honest Injun, I didn't make out what he said. Mebbe now he struck a whopper of a trout, and was giving one of his whoops. You all know how excited Steve does get if anything out of the way happens."

"L-l-listen!" cried Toby Jncklin, jumping to his feet. "D-d-didn't it sound like he was yelpin' help?"

"Just what it seemed like to me!" exclaimed Max. "Something may have happened to Steve, because he's always getting himself in trouble. Come along, fellows, and we'll soon find out. There, he's whooping it up again."

And this time every one of the trio of running boys could plainly detect something approaching agony in the thrilling cry of "Help, oh! hurry up, fellows! Help!"

CHAPTER II

GRIPPED BY A GIANT'S UNSEEN HANDS

That Max, Bandy-legs and Toby all kept their wits about them was manifest. Their actions had made this clear enough, for each of the trio before starting "on the jump," as Bandy-legs described it, had made sure to pick up something that, according to his mind, was apt to be needed. Max, for instance, had snatched a rope that hung from a broken branch of the tree, and which one of the boys had fetched along simply because "a rope often comes in mighty handy for lots of things besides a hanging bee." On his part Toby had stooped down and possessed himself of the camp hatchet; if it proved that Steve was being attacked by a bobcat he fancied he could make pretty good use of such a tool in an emergency. Bandy-legs, true to his hunter instinct, made out to secure the only gun which had been brought with them on the trip.

As they ran wildly in the direction from whence those appeals for assistance still came, louder than ever, every fellow was straining his vision to be the first to discover what it could be that was causing Steve to let out such alarming whoops.

They did not have very far to go before suddenly all of them discovered the object of their solicitude. He seemed to be standing nearly waist-deep in the stream, and still holding on to his tough little steel rod.

"Oh! shucks!" gasped Bandy-legs, almost out of breath from his violent exertions, "he's only struck a mud turtle, or something like that, and wants us to come and see. It's a burning shame to give us all such a scare over a measly turtle."

"B-b-bet you it's a w-w-woppin' b-b-big fish!" ejaculated Toby.

"Keep on running!" snapped Max. "He needs help, and in a hurry, too!"

This sort of talk amazed both the others. So far as they could see Steve stood there quite alone. They looked again but could see no savage animal attacking their comrade; nor was there any vast disturbance in the water, as though some marine monster might be trying to drag him down; besides, such things as alligators or sharks were utterly unknown up here in the Adirondacks.

"But, Max, he's all right, as far as I can see," expostulated Bandy-legs, in reality unwilling to keep up that violent exertion just to please some silly whim on the part of the fisherman, who, like as not, would give them the laugh after they came up puffing and blowing like porpoises.

"Look again," snapped Max. "Don't you see how deep he's in? Pretty nearly up to his waist, isn't he?"

"That's all right," said Bandy-legs, "but if the silly has gone and waded deeper than he meant to, why don't he just turn around and walk out again?"

"Because he can't!" Max told him, still running.

"Hey! w-w-what's hindering him!" stammered Toby, thrilled by this new mystery that had so suddenly dawned upon them.

"The sand's got too tight a grip on him," cried Max, "and he's sinking deeper all the time!"

"Oh! thunder, it's quicksand, then!" exploded Bandy-legs.

Having now the key to the enigma explaining Steve's strange action, as well as his queer antics while floundering about out there in the little stream, both boys could easily see that May evidently spoke the truth. So those envious Spanish courtiers found it easy to balance an egg on end, after Columbus showed them how to do the trick.

In another half minute they arrived on the shore of the little stream. Steve out there, with the shallow water coming now up almost to his waist, greeted their arrival with a sickly grin.

"Sorry to bother you, boys," he said, "but seems like I've gone and got into a nasty pickle. Please yank me out of this, won't you?"

Impetuous Bandy-legs was about to instantly start forward when Max gripped him by the arm.

"Don't be foolish, Bandy-legs," he told the other, severely. "You'd only get yourself in the same boat, if you stood there and tried to drag Steve out; and two would be harder to take care of than one."

"But say, don't be *too* slow about starting something, will you?" urged Steve, once again looking nervous. "Why, I'm sinking right along, I tell you. Every time I try to get one foot up t' other goes down three inches further, because I have to bear all my weight on it. This is no laughing matter, boys. I'll be swallowed up before your eyes soon if you don't get busy. Max, you ought to know how to extricate a fellow from the quicksand!"

"There are lots of ways in which it can be done," the other told him, meanwhile measuring distances with his eye, as though he already had a plan in mind. "If when you first discovered that you were sinking you had thrown yourself sideways, and started to crawl or roll, regardless of how wet you got, you might have made it, for in that way you'd have presented more of your body to the action of the sand. Then a mattress could be made from branches, weeds or any old thing, that would bear the weight of one or two of us. But I've got even a better scheme than that to work."

"Please hurry!" pleaded the imprisoned boy.

"Keep cool, Steve," advised Max, "because there's positively no danger, now that we're on deck."

"But tell me what you mean to do, Max?" continued Steve.

"Make use of this rope, which you see I just happened to fetch along," explained the other, holding up the article in question. "It's going to save time, too, because one of us would have had to run back to camp, and that must mean delay. You're deep enough in as it is, I guess."

"A whole lot deeper than is pleasant, I tell you," Steve instantly added. "Why, at the rate it's sucking me down I guess in less'n a quarter of an hour the water would be up to my chin. And then, oh! fellows, just imagine how I'd feel when it began to cover my mouth. You're not going away, I hope, Max?"

This last almost frantic cry was caused by a movement on the part of the one on whom poor Steve's hopes most depended.

"I'm going to shin up this big tree that sends a limb out right over your head, don't you see, Steve?" Max told him, reassuringly. "Once I get above you and we'll make good use of this rope of mine. The limb will act as a lever, and when the boys get to pulling at the other end of the rope you've just *got* to come out, that's all there is about it."

"Hurrah! that's the ticket!" shouted Bandy-legs, seeing the game now for the first time. "Steve, you're as good as landed. Bless that old rope, it's already proved worth its weight in gold." Steve watched operations anxiously. Despite the positive assurance conveyed in these words from his chums, the terrible grip of that clinging sand made him cold with apprehension. He imagined all sorts of things, from the rope breaking under the sudden and terrible strain, to his arms being drawn from their sockets in the battle between the tenacious sand and the muscular ability of the two boys ashore.

When Max managed to reach a point directly above the one in peril, straddling the friendly limb as only a nimble boy could do, he quickly fashioned a slip-noose at one end of the rope. This he lowered until Steve could snatch it, which he did with all the eagerness shown by the drowning man who clutches at a straw.

"Fix the noose under your arms, Steve," directed the master of ceremonies, calmly enough, though possibly Max was more excited than he chose to let the other see, "and get the knot around so it will be exactly in front. Then, when I give the word for the boys to commence heaving, you work both legs as hard as ever you can. It's going to help, more or less, you know. I can't do much up here, in the way of pulling, for I'd lose my balance; but make up your mind we're meaning to yank you out of that in a jiffy, Steve."

"Oh! I hope so, Max, I surely hope so!"

Everything was soon ready. Steve had complied with the directions, and now awaited the issue with all the fortitude he could command. Afterwards perhaps Steve might sometime or other even laugh, as he remembered how scared he was; but just then, with the difficulty still unadjusted, it was not at all humorous.

"Ready, everybody?" called out Max.

Receiving an affirmative reply from three pairs of lips, he went on to say:

"Then get busy, pulling! Make it a steady haul, and no jerks, or you'll hurt Steve more than is necessary. Steady there, Bandy-legs, no hurry, remember—just a regular increasing pull! Good enough, boys!"

Steve had obeyed instructions, and by the way he worked both feet as soon as he felt the strain one might think he was practicing swimming lessons. It must have given him more or less physical pain to feel the terrible drag of the rope under his arms, but he shut his teeth hard together, and kept back a groan.

"Now rest a bit, Toby and Bandy-legs!" called out Max. "How about it, Steve—you moved some, didn't you?"

"Yes yes, quite a little, Max!" cried the other. "Please get busy again right away. I'm sick of staying in this old quicksand!"

He still clung tenaciously to his steel fishing rod, as though he meant that it should share his fate. Once more the team ashore started in. Now their task seemed lighter, as though, having succeeded in dragging their chum up several inches, with his whole weight now suspended by the rope, the job was going to be finished in short order.

Soon Steve, crowing joyously, was drawn completely out of the water. He gave this a last suggestive kick and then dangled there in midair, spinning around like a teetotum.

"Hand me your rod, Steve," commanded Max. "Then use your arms and pull yourself up on the limb. After that you can easily hunch along like I do, and get to the main trunk. It's all over but the shouting, Steve; and you can consider yourself pretty lucky to get off as easily as you do, with a pair of wet trousers."

"I'm thankful enough, Max, you can make sure of that," said the other, carrying out the suggestion, and thus freeing both hands for the task of mounting to the friendly limb.

Before long he had reached the ground, where his three chums each gravely shook hands with him. Steve was already getting back his nerve, that had been under a severe strain.

"But anyway I did have bully good luck pulling out fat trout, boys," he told them. "You can pick up a dozen along this side of the stream. Fact is, it was such splendid fun that I just stood too long in one place, catching them and tossing the beauties ashore; and so when I tried to move, why, I couldn't to save my life. It felt like a giant had gripped both feet, and was holding me down. The more I tried the worse it got. Whee! I would have been pretty badly scared if no one was near by, I own up to that."

Perhaps the others mentally considered that as it was, Steve had looked a "good deal concerned" at the time of their arrival; but not wishing to harrow his feelings any further just then they kept this to themselves; though Bandy-legs did give Toby a suggestive wink, to which the other replied in like kind.

It was found upon gathering the trophies of Steve's skill as an angler that they had quite enough for a meal; consequently Steve announced that he guessed he needn't start in again with rod and hook and grub.

All of them were soon busily engaged in fixing up the camp. Since they had thought it best not to try and fetch a heavy tent along with them they knew it would be necessary to construct some such brush shanty shelter every night unless they could find a convenient ledge under which a camp could be made. But all of these boys had often slept under the stars, with the heavens for a canopy overhead, so that they did not feel at all worried over the circumstance.

As the sun sank lower and lower toward the horizon the camp began to assume a comfortable air. The brush shelter had been finished, and pronounced equal to any they had ever built before. It might not prove wholly rain-proof, but as for keeping off the dew, and protecting them against the chilly night air, it offered them "all the comforts of home," as Steve put it.

Then supper was started, a fire having been built after the most approved method in vogue among guides and hunters of long experience. Indeed, Max and his companions were far from being green to the ways of the woods. They had learned heaps through their many camping experiences; and some time before a visit to an old trapper had initiated them into dozens of secrets of the craft that would never be forgotten.[1]

Again the talk was of the strange mission that had brought them up to the Adirondacks. Bandy-legs could not seem to get over his belief that they were bound to have all their trouble for their pains.

"What sort of a clue have we got to work on for a starter, fellows, tell me?" he went on to say, just as they were starting in to enjoy the supper that had been supervised by a trio of eager cooks, all as hungry as boys could well be, and continue to exist. "All we know is that when this boy, Roland Chase, left Sagamere, almost two years back, he was a sickly, white-faced chap, and with only one decent trait about him, which was his love for outdoors; though up to then it had been mostly a *yearning*, because they wouldn't let him get away from the house much on account of his delicate constitution. Well, we're looking for some such chap; but up to now we haven't got on his track."

[1] "With Trapper Jim in the North Woods."

"But hold on, Bandy-legs," expostulated Steve, "you forget that we did hear about a boy that answered that description, though nobody seemed to know his name. He was sometimes seen in the company of a half-drunken old guide named Shanks somewhere around Mount Tom district. And now we've come up this way in the hope of crossing his trail. Not that I've got much expectation myself that we'll be sure to find this same; Roland, who turns out to be a sort of will-o'-the-wisp to us; but since his old aunt was so kind as to finance this expedition, why we're bound to do all we can to make it a blooming success, that's what."

"Well," commented Max, who seemed to be the most confident one of the quartette, "remember, if we fail to make connections it'll be the first time on record that we've really been stumped. I don't believe in hard-luck stories. As a rule success comes only to those who deserve it. And we've still got most of that two weeks' vacation ahead of us, to hunt around for Roland Chase."

Somehow Max always seemed to say things calculated to make his chums feel more satisfied. It is a mighty good thing to have a real optimist in camp, especially when the weather gets bad, and everything else seems to go wrong. Even Bandy-legs took on a more cheerful air, and brightened up after hearing Max say this. They had more or less reason to feel proud of the record they had made in the past, so far as accomplishing things went. And the people around Carson would be apt to tell any one inquiring about Max and his cronies that they had actually done several exceedingly smart things, and were boys far above the average.

The supper was voted a huge success, and never had fish been fried a more delicious brown than those in the pan. Perhaps Steve entertained a private opinion of his own, to the effect that never had a higher price been paid for a mess of fish than he offered up when he found himself made a prisoner of the unseen giant residing under the quicksands; but all the same, Steve devoured his share of the fish as smartly as the next one. He doubtless felt that he deserved having a feast, after his adventure in supplying the materials.

They were almost through eating, and feeling particularly well satisfied, as is usually the case, when the appetite has been taken care of, when Toby Jucklin was seen to be staring straight ahead.

"What ails you, Toby?" demanded Steve, discovering the mysterious actions of the other. "Think you see a ghost; or was it a 'coon whisked past, smelling our fine spread here? Speak up, can't you, and tell us?"

Toby managed to find his tongue, and as usual when excited made quite a mess of his explanation.

"W-w-why, y-y-you s-s-see, I—t-that is, there's s-s-somebody—oh! look for yourselves and you'll understand quicker'n I c'n tell you!"

Sometimes Toby seemed to become so provoked with his ungovernable vocal organs that he would get angry, and wind up by speaking as plainly as the next one.

But before then Max, and perhaps the other pair in the bargain, had discovered a figure advancing slowly toward them. Eagerly Bandy-legs stared. Perhaps he began to already entertain a wild hope that the newcomer would prove to be the very boy whom they had come so far to find; but if this were so he must have almost immediately discovered his mistake, for the other was a sun-burned and wind-tanned lad, sturdily built, and apparently the son of some woods guide; for he carried a gun, and was dressed in rough though serviceable khaki trousers and blue flannel shirt.

CHAPTER III

OBED GRIMES BOBS UP

"Howdy, strangers!" said the other, as he slowly approached the spot where Max and his three chums still sat around the fire, feasting on their spread. "I happened to see yer blaze, and guessed I'd drop in to see who yah might be. 'Taint often anybody comes up this way, though to be sure thar was two gentlemen fishin' hereabouts last summer."

Somehow Max liked his manner of speech. He also thought he could detect something like a love for humor in those sparkling eyes.

"Sit down, and have a bite with us, won't you?" he remarked, making a suggestive movement with his hand, as though calling attention to the fact that there was still plenty of room on the log which he and Toby Jucklin had occupied in common. "Sorry the trout's given out, but we've got plenty of other grub, and be sure you're welcome."

The sturdy woods boy was looking them over. Bandy-legs, suspicious as usual, rather took umbrage at this action. He eyed the newcomer as though not yet quite willing to echo the warm invitation accorded him by Max. But Steve was already getting an extra tin-cup for coffee; and fortunately there still remained an abundant supply of the amber fluid in the capacious pot.

Apparently the newcomer had determined that it would be prudent for him to comply with the invitation thus cordially given. So he sat down and made himself at home. Up there in the woods there exists a genuine hospitality that never hesitates to extend the right hand of fellowship to any straggler who chances to enter the camp. There seems to be something in the healthy ozone of the wilderness that makes all men comrades for the time being. The latchstring is always out in camp; and never does an appeal for help go disregarded.

Max proceeded to immediately introduce himself and his three chums by name. He of course mentioned the fact that they came from a town named Carson, situated far away from that region; but then of course the woods boy could never have heard of such a place before. Still, his eyebrows arched, and he seemed to once again observe his entertainers with fresh interest; but then when Max Hastings chose to exert himself to make a favorable impression every one fell under his spell.

And when Bandy-legs, Toby and Steve noticed that Max did not think fit to say a single word about the queer mission which had brought them to the mountains they too concluded that it would be just as well not to be too hasty about telling all their business to a stranger. A little later on, perhaps, when they came to become better acquainted with the other, they might ply him with questions in order to find out if he chanced to know such a weakly looking fellow as Roland Chase.

Of course after that it was up to the other to tell them whom he was. He did not have any hesitation, from which Steve concluded there could be no reason for keeping his identity a secret.

"Course I got a name, too, even if it ain't *quite* so scrumptuous as yours. But Obed Grimes suits me just as well, and it ain't never kept me from eatin' three square meals a day—when I could get 'em," he told them, soberly, though that odd little gleam in his eyes mystified Max somewhat.

"I suppose you live around this section, then, Obed?" he remarked, as he cleaned out the frying-pan that had contained the ham and eggs—the latter having been carried all the way from the last small village they passed through, and which supply would doubtless be the last they might enjoy for a long time to come.

"Oh! yes, thar's a plenty of Grimeses up this way," the other replied, promptly. "Fact is, the Grimeses are a big family, all told. Thar's Grandad Grimes to start with, and he's going on ninety now; then there's Uncle Hiram, Uncle Silas, Uncle Job, Uncle Sephus, Uncle

Nicodemus, and a whole lot more; besides Aunt Rebecca, Aunt Sophia, Aunt Hetebel, and—glory to goodness, I could sit here for ten minutes and string out the names of the grimeses there are in the mountains; but say I'm *awful* hungry, and you'll excuse me if I get busy with this fine grub. The other names will keep till next time, I reckon."

"Whew! it must feel funny to belong to such a big family," remarked Steve, who did not happen to have any close relatives himself.

"Oh! shucks! none of 'em ever bother about *me* any," said the boy, as well as he could with his mouth stuffed of the ham and bread, which he presently washed down with a copious draught of hot coffee. "They just know that Obed he c'n take good care o' hisself."

Bandy-legs began to show a rising interest in the other. His suspicions were beginning to give way under the genial ways of the said Obed. That smile on the dusky face of the visitor in the camp had commenced to get its work in. By degrees perhaps Bandy-legs might even come to like Obed Grimes; though, truth to tell, he had always despised that last name, for a boy answering to it had once treated Bandy-legs in a most humiliating fashion, and this still rankled in his memory, although years had fled since the occurrence.

"Do you mean from that, Obed," he went on to remark "that you're all alone up here in the woods near old Mount Tom? Haven't you any of the other Grimeses along with you?"

The boy shook his head in the negative, and grinned again. Max was trying to study him, and he found the task one well worthy of his best efforts. In the beginning he determined that Obed was no ordinary chap, but possessed of sterling characteristics. He waited for the conversation to get further along, confident that the other had a surprise up his sleeve which he might condescend to share with them, after he had become fully satisfied they were to be trusted, and that he could look upon them in the light of friends.

"Nary a Grimes 'cept me inside o' twenty miles o' here, and that's a fact," he assured Bandy-legs, after finishing his drinking. "Fact is, most o' the family don't know jest where I'm at; and say, between us, I ain't a carin' about tellin' 'em."

That looked a bit singular, Bandy-legs thought. His suspicions returned again, though with diminished force; for somehow he could not look into that frank and even merry face of the woods boy and actually believe he was "off-color" in any way.

"But what do you do with yourself all alone, I'd like to know?" burst out impetuous Steve. "Are you making a living playing at guide for parties of tourists, or fishermen and hunters? And, say, you don't mean to tell me you stay all alone up in this wilderness right through the winter?"

Obed Grimes nodded his head cheerfully.

"I ain't got any choice in the matter, yuh see," he told them, mysteriously; "just *got* to stay. Why, it would bust the hull business to smash if I 'lowed myself to skip out, even for a week or two. I'm tied down to it, that's right."

Bandy-legs exchanged a significant look Toby Jucklin. He scratched his head with the air of one who found himself up against a hard, knotty problem. Apparently, if the stranger in camp was trying to mystify them, he had already succeeded in tangling up the wits of Bandy-legs completely.

Max continued to sit there and take it all in. There was no need of his saying anything so long as the other fellows had embarked on the task of drawing Obed out and learning just what he was doing to keep him marooned up there summer and winter, like a regular old recluse, or woodchuck.

"But there must be heaps and heaps of snow here winters," suggested Steve; "and I'd think you'd find it pretty hard getting about."

"Oh! not so bad when you have snow-shoes" Obed told him, with a shrug of his shoulders, and another attack on the contents of his tin panninkin.

"'Course not," Steve hastened to say, as though he had guessed that this would be the answer. "But when the law is on the deer and partridges it must be hard to keep to a regular diet of trout. I c'n stand them for a while; but in the end I'd get sick of the smell of 'em cooking."

"Oh! I have plenty of good grub along," chuckled Obed. "I was on my way home at the time I glimpsed your fire; and bein' full o' wonder concernin' who could be around these diggings right now I crept up to spy on ye. But say, soon's I glimpsed your crowd, and saw that you was only a bunch o' boys, why I felt easier, 'cause I knew then you couldn't mean to bother me any."

Now that sounded queer again, Bandy-legs thought. Why should any one take the trouble to "bother" Obed Grimes, unless, indeed, he had been doing something that he hadn't ought to, and hence expected to be visited sooner or later by emissaries of the law, possibly in the shape of angry game wardens?

All sorts of strange thoughts flashed through that active brain of the boy with the bowed legs. He wondered whether Obed could be a desperate young criminal. Had his family, those excellent Grimes of whom he had spoken in such proud accents, cast him out as altogether beyond hope? Bandy-legs could hardly think this when he looked again into that face, and caught the gleam of those merry orbs. No, Obed might be a *peculiar* sort of fellow, but really there did not seem to be much of guile in his make-up; if it turned out to be so, then he, Bandy-legs, was ready to call himself a mighty poor reader of character.

So he, too, relapsed into temporary silence and let Steve carry on the interrogations; which the said Steve considered himself very well qualified to do since he aspired in his secret soul to some fine day study to be a lawyer.

"But why should anybody want to bother you, Obed?" he asked. "To hear you talk in that way a fellow would think you had a lot of enemies hanging around, trying the best they knew how to give you trouble."

"Well, I ain't had any mix-up ever since I've been here," admitted the other, with a slight frown crossing his face; "but lately I got wind o' some news that's worried me a heap. Fact is, I'm afraid I'm goin' to be right smart bothered with a bunch o' thieves who'd like to *steal* my outfit from me!"

Steve fairly gasped. He could not make head or tail of what the other was so deliberately telling him. Max, listening, and watching that expressive face of Obed, secretly believed the newcomer was purposely drawing Steve on, meaning to surprise him when finally he chose to explain it all. So Max did not attempt to interfere, but let things go on as they were doing, satisfied that the answer to the conundrum would soon come.

"Steal your outfit from you?" echoed Steve, when he could catch his breath; "do you mean that you're carrying on some sort of business, then, up here in the woods?"

"Reckon that's about right, Steve," Obed replied, and his familiar use of the other's name could be easily explained by that spirit of "free masonry" that exists among all boys. "I've got a business, which looks like it was goin' to pan out right decent, and make me some money in the bargain. That's why they're meanin' to rob me, I guess; anyhow, it hinges on that same thing. And I thought you might be that crowd first, but I soon saw I was mistaken, and that you'd be my friend."

"But what sort of business is it you're in, Obed?" asked Steve, boldly.

"Me? Oh! I'm only a farmer," confessed the other, chuckling as he spoke.

"A farmer!" echoed Steve, looking blank; "but how could anybody steal your ground away, or carry off your crops, I'd like to know?"

"Why, yuh don't jest understand, Steve. I ain't no regular hayseed. I'm a fur farmer, you see; and you could carry my crop of fox pelts away easy enough on your own back!"

CHAPTER IV

BANDY-LEGS SUSPECTS

Max Hastings smiled. He at the same time drew a breath of relief, satisfied to know that his first impression of the sturdy looking young chap was confirmed, and convinced that the said Obed Grimes must be the right sort of fellow.

Steve and Bandy-legs fairly gasped, as though they had received a real shock. At the same time the eyes of the former glistened with newly-awakened interest.

"A fur farmer, do you say, Obed? And raising foxes for the market, are you?" he burst out with, delightedly. "Now, I've read a heap about that sort of thing in the papers and magazines, but I never thought I'd actually run across anybody that had the nerve and confidence to go into it as a business. And you say you're making good, are you, Obed? That's fine!"

"I've turned my 'tention to raisin' real black foxes, first thing," explained the other, with a touch of genuine pride in his manner, Max could easily see; "and if the try turns out as profitable as I reckon she promises to be, why, then, I'm figgerin' on tryin' to raise mink and marten and sech other furs as fetch top-notch prices."

"Then I guess you must have trapped all sorts of wild animals before now, Obed?" suggested Steve, eagerly, "so you know their habits to a fraction; because, of course, only one who is posted in that direction could ever hope to make a success of a fur farm."

Obed grinned and nodded his head.

"Oh! I reckon I'm up a little bit in all sech things," he said airily enough. "And after all, it ain't so *very* hard to raise foxes. I was afraid fust off it might be what they told me, that blacks ain't to be relied on to breed true to strain, but shucks! I've got some cubs that are dandies. Wait till you see 'em, boys."

That sounded as though, sooner or later, Obed meant to have them visit his fur farm, and see with their own eyes what he had been doing. Bandy-legs, skeptical once more, told himself he only hoped the whole thing might not turn out to be a myth, and that the said Obed himself prove to be a deception and a fraud.

"I understand that the pelts of black foxes are worth a whole lot of money," remarked Steve; "fact is, we know that to be so, because we once had such a skin given to us by a man who made a business of trapping."

"It all depends on the quality of the pelt," explained Obed. "Some ain't worth as much as three hundred dollars, because they've got defects, yuh see. Then again a real fine skin has fetched as much as thirty-six hundred dollars in London markets."

Evidently, Obed was well posted, at any rate, whether he really had such a fur farm of his own or not, Bandy-legs concluded. And then he again allowed himself to give imagination free rein, and for a time even looked on Obed as the essence of truth, doubly distilled.

Sitting there by the fire, which one of he boys replenished every little while, Obed told them many very interesting things connected with that strange farm of his. All this in his odd vernacular which Max tried to get the hang of, in order to judge whether it signified that the country boy lacked an education or not. He continued to be more or less mystified, however, though concluding that Obed was just one of those customary country boys often run across on farms who take especial delight in joking and playing little tricks which they consider humorous.

"But he isn't at all bad, I'll stake everything on that" Max also told himself, as he sat and listened to the really interesting descriptions given by the other of his successes, and first failures along the difficult line of breeding foxes in captivity, with scores of things against him, which had to be overcome.

An hour passed by in this manner. When Max saw their visitor showing signs as if he meant to leave them, he took a hand in the conversation, which up to then had been almost wholly monopolized by Bandy-legs, Steve and the woods boy.

"It's very kind of you to invite us over to inspect this wonderful little fur farm of yours, Obed," he went on to say; "but you'll have to give us directions how we can get there, unless you mean to accept our offer of a blanket by the fire here tonight, when we could go along with you in the morning."

Obed looked sober.

"I'd like to stay longer with you, boys," he hastened to say, as though he really meant it, "but I ought tuh be gettin' back home. Thar's some duties waitin' for me to look after. And then I ain't quite easy in my mind 'bout them two fellers that's up here in the woods. They ain't meanin' to do any shootin', even if they have got Lem Scott along as a guide, and he the meanest skunk in the hull county, lots o' folks do say, and a poacher in the bargain that the wardens are layin' to grab one o' these fine days. Now I'll jest up and tell yuh how to get to my place. It's as easy as water runnin' down-hill."

He entered into explicit directions, and Max pinned them in his memory. In fact, Obed simply told them to follow the stream up three miles until they came to a bunch of seven birch trees on the right-hand bank. There they were to pick up a trail they would find, follow it half a mile, and at that they would see a cabin under the hemlocks and pines, which would be his humble home woods.

"We've got it all down pat, Obed," said Steve, "and like as not you'll see the bunch of us trailing along there some time tomorrow morning. I've always been crazy to see a fur farm, after reading so much about them, and you bet I don't mean to let this chance slip by me."

Max now thought it time to make a few inquiries himself. He wanted to ask Obed whether he had ever run across a boy by the name of Roland Chase, a sickly looking chap in the bargain. It might possible to pick up a clue in this way; and they had reached a point where they could not afford to let any opportunity for acquiring information get past them.

In order to pursue this course, however, Max realized that it would be necessary to enter into some sort of explanation concerning the nature of the peculiar errand that had tempted them to come to the Adirondacks.

"I want to ask you a question or two, Obed," he began, "but first of all I ought to tell you what brings us here."

Accordingly, Max proceeded to explain how the school had be closed for two or more weeks in early October, and what a singular thing came about to tempt them into taking an outing. He was watching the woods boy at the time he first mentioned Mrs. Hopewell, and spoke the name of Roland Chase; but if the other gave any unusual signs of interest, Max failed to catch the same. Still, Obed was listening with all his might, and it seemed as though the unusual story of the inheritance that was to be given to the said Roland in case he made good, interested him.

Max in this manner explained just why he and his three chums had accepted the generous offer of the elderly lady, so deeply concerned over the welfare of her nephew Boland, that she was ready to spend almost any reasonable sum in order to at least learn that the poor boy was alive, and in fairly decent health.

They had been told to assure him, in case they ever managed to locate the elusive Roland, that he should not worry because of not being able to comply with the absurd conditions of Uncle Jerry's ridiculous will; because she had enough of this world's goods for both, and she meant to leave it all to him, Roland; so she begged him to come back to her, and live his own life again, even though he had spent the last penny of his two-thousand-dollar legacy, and was as poor as Job's turkey.

All this made an interesting story, and must have amused the woods boy more or less, because Max knew how to put considerable pathos in it. Obed sat there shading his eyes with his hand to keep the glow of the fire from dazzling him. Occasionally he would interrupt to ask some natural question, which made Max think he was taking a fair amount of interest in the account.

"What I wanted to ask you," concluded Max, "was whether you'd ever happened to run across this same Roland Chase in the mountains. We heard about a fellow answering his description who was seen in company with a dissipated guide named Shanks. I thought perhaps you might help us out, Obed."

Obed looked him straight in the face.

"So far as I knows on, Max," he went on to say, seriously, "I ain't never met any feller like yuh say face to face. About that man Shanks, I know he's said to be a tough un. I saw him some months back down at Sawyer's Forks, and by hokey! now that you mention it, thar *was* a sickly lookin' young feller along with him then; but say, his name was Bob Jenks, or somethin' like that, and not Roland Chase."

"Oh! well, so far as that goes," said Max, "he may have changed his name. Some people think nothing of sailing under false colors; and if it turns out that Roland has taken up with such a disreputable character as this drunken guide seems to be, I don't wonder at him wanting to hide his identity. So you think you must be going home, do you, Obed?"

"Yep," the other observed, gaining his feet. "And I wanter to thank all o' ye for givin' me sech a pleasant evenin'. I ain't had sech a good time this long while back. But then the Grimeses all are 'customed to roughin' it. Granddad used to be away all by hisself for as much as two years, trappin' up in Canada. It's in the blood, I reckon. Now, yuh mean to drop in, and visit me, don't ye? I'll be expectin' yuh, and have something to eat awarmin', though course I ain't a good cook like you fellers, as has had so much experience. So long, boys!"

He waved them a cheerful goodbye, once more smiled at each in turn, whirled on his heel, and was gone, seeming to vanish in the shadows of the nearby woods like "a wisp of smoke when the wind strikes it," as Steve remarked.

After the departure of their guest, it was only natural that he should be the subject of conversation about the fire as the four chums lay there taking things easy.

"Max, honest to goodness now," Bandy-legs remarked, "do you really take any stock in that fairy story he told us about an imaginary fur farm? It struck me Obed is givin to yarnin' just for the love of it. All that stuff about his relatives may have been true, and again only nonsense. It's my opinion there isn't any Granddad Grimes, or Uncle Hiram, Nicodemus and so forth. He grinned like everything when he was reeling those names off so slick. Yes, he was stringing us, I bet you."

"W-w-why," burst out Toby just then, "who wouldn't have to s-s-snicker when he had a w-w-whole lot of relations with such f-f-funny names! It'd make me grin from ear to ear every time I h-h-happened to think of 'em. You're the greatest hand to s-s-suspect anybody I ever s-s-saw, Bandy-legs. Now, I want you to k-k-know that I think Obed the s-s-straight g-g-goods, and I'm taking a heap of s-s-stock in seeing that bully f-f-fur f-f-farm of his tomorrow; ain't you, Max?"

"Certainly I am," replied the other, without a second's hesitation. "In the first place, Bandy-legs, you must understand that nobody could talk so interestingly on a subject unless he knew a lot about it. He told us a dozen things about fur farming that I never heard before."

"Huh! and perhaps nobody else ever heard of them either, Max," grunted the far from satisfied Bandy-legs.

"Nothing will ever satisfy him except he sees those kit foxes with his own eyes," asserted Steve, almost indignantly, "handles them with his own paws, and asks every little critter whether he really belongs to Obed Grimes. Bandy-legs is the worst Doubting Thomas going, when the fit comes on him."

Even this sort of talk did not convince the objector.

"Say what you will, fellows," Bandy-legs went on, stubbornly, "there's a wheen of queer things connected with this same Obed Grimes, and I won't take that back till he shows us his wonderful old farm, where he raises black foxes for the fur market. Stop and think how mysteriously he popped in on us, will you? Why, he as much as owned up that he had been spying on us for a long time. If Toby here hadn't discovered him peeking, and pointed that way, chances are he wouldn't have shown up at all. Now, what made him snoop around our camp like that?"

"Say, didn't he explain all that just as straight as a die?" objected Steve, who seemed to have conceived quite a fancy for Obed Grimes, the woods boy. "He told us he had reason to fear some unscrupulous fellows were hanging around this region and meaning to steal his pets when they got half a chance. That was why he wanted to watch, and make sure we didn't belong to the same crowd."

"Oh! yes, a likely story, too," continued Bandy-legs, with a sneer. "Why should anybody want to rob a poor boy who was trying to earn his living by farming, even if it was furs he raised instead of grain or hogs or stock?"

"Why, you poor ninny, the reason is as plain as the nose on your face, Bandy-legs, and that's not invisible by a big sight. When a black fox pelt will fetch a thousand dollars, more or less, and can't well be traced once it gets mixed with other pelts, it stands to reason that any thief would want to steal it. As to your doubting that there are any other people up in this section, you seem to forget, Bandy-legs, that around noon today we sighted a plain smoke some miles away, which we opined must have been made by some advance hunters, waiting for the law to be off deer. Well, why couldn't it have been the people Obed says he fears, who made that smoke? Now, for my part, I believe every word Obed Grimes said. He's the straight goods every time, and you can see it in his eye, for he looks you direct in the face."

Thereupon, Bandy-legs, as though realizing that he had raised a hornet's nest about his ears, deemed it the part of discretion to shrug his shoulders after the manner of one who, "convinced against his will is of the same opinion still."

"We'll let the subject drop, Steve," he said, hastily. "It ain't worth quarreling over. The proof of the pudding is in the eating of it; and tomorrow we'll *know* what's what. But remember, if it turns out that we've been bamboozled, don't blame me, because I've warned you all."

"If we had a chill from every warning you've sprung on us, Bandy-legs," Steve told him, witheringly, "why, say, we'd have gone all to pieces long before now. You're a regular old bad-weather prognosticator, that's what you are."

"That's right, get to calling names. It's a habit with people who know they are in the wrong," grumbled Bandy-legs; but, nevertheless, he "drew within his shell," and said nothing further about Obed Grimes or his suspicions concerning the same.

CHAPTER V

PACKING OVER THE "CARRY"

Later on the conversation began to lag. Steve was noticed drowsily nodding his head in a suggestive way; and then after a sudden start he would look around aggressively, as if to remark: "who said I was sleepy?" but within three minutes he would be at it again.

In fact all of the boys were really tired out. The day's tramp had been a difficult one, even for fellows accustomed to such things; and those regular Adirondack packs, with a band crossing the forehead in the usual way, had seemed doubly heavy before they decided to stop for the night.

Of course there were sounds to be heard all around them, but "familiarity breeds contempt," and from Max down they were all accustomed to hearing similar noises whenever they spent nights in the open. The owl would whinny or hoot according to his species; the loon send forth his agonizing and weird shriek from some distant lake; a fox might bark sharply and fretfully, or two quarrelsome 'coons dispute over a bit of food they had discovered— all this went with the camping business, and indeed it would have seemed odd to those boys had the usual accompaniment been missing.

"Well, what's the use of our staying up longer?" Max finally announced in an authoritative fashion, after Steve had almost jerked his neck awry for about the seventh time, with one of those spasmodic movements. "Our blankets are calling to us, boys; let's turn in."

There was no negative vote recorded, for every one seemed ready to call it a day, and quit. Max took it upon himself to look after the fire. Plenty of wood had been gathered to last until morning, and then some; for, as the night air was beginning to feel pretty sharp, it was concluded to keep the fire going.

"I'll look out for that part," said Max. "I generally wake up just so many times during the night when I'm in camp, and it's no trouble for me to crawl out and toss another stick on the fire. So forget it, fellows, will you?"

Apparently the others took him at his word, for not another sign of any of them was seen while night lasted. Once they snuggled down in their warm comfortable blankets, they must have become "dead to the world," as Steve aptly termed it.

Several times while the night held sway a figure would crawl noiselessly out of the crude brush shanty shelter, and place another lot of wood upon the dwindling fire, thus keeping it going for another spell of several hours. Of course this was Max, who really liked to take an observation concerning the state of the weather, note the changed positions of the heavenly bodies, so that he could figure on the passage of time; and then once more creep into the folds of his blanket to again fall into a deep sleep.

So the night passed.

Nothing occurred to disturb its serenity. The little four-footed woods folks doubtless prowled all around the boys' camp, eyeing the glimmering fire with wonder and distrust, for it could not be a familiar sight to any of them, since mankind seldom visited this inaccessible region so far removed from the track of ordinary travel. Some of the more daring among them, venturesome 'coons or 'possums perhaps, may even have invaded the precincts of the charmed circle, searching with their keen little noses for traces of castaway food; but, if so, their presence did not disturb the sleepers within that shelter.

So morning came on apace, and presently from the brush shanty one after another of the fellows came creeping forth, to stretch and yawn and finally hasten their dressing, for the frosty air nipped fingers and toes quite lustily.

They were in no particular hurry, and breakfast therefore was undertaken in the best of humor, with plenty of time given to its preparation. Everybody seemed to be in the best of humors, and his good sleep must have smoothed even the spirit of the fretful Bandy-legs, for he no longer grumbled or found fault. Perhaps, as so frequently happened, he was secretly ashamed of having shown such a suspicious and argumentative disposition on the preceding evening, and meant to make amends for it by an unusually cheery manner.

It was determined to "break camp" soon after the matin meal had been comfortably dispatched. This did not promise to be an extraordinary feat, since they were trying to go light-handed on this expedition, and did not have many of their ordinary "traps" along, from a tent down to certain cooking utensils that had been deemed too heavy for "toting" mile after mile into the wilderness.

It makes a whole lot of difference just how fellows mean to go, when laying out the impedimenta for a trip. If a wagon or a boat is available, all sorts of things may as well be taken along, so as to insure the maximum of comfort; but when it is known in the beginning that all they are meaning to use must be packed every mile of the way on the back of the campers, then it is high time to cut down the list to the last fraction, so far as weight and bulk are concerned.

Max and his chums had reduced this down to a real science. For instance, having a comfortable balance at the bank, thanks to their thrift in the past,[2] money did not enter into their calculations at all. Consequently, they had purchased a complete little outfit of aluminum cooking vessels that nested within each other and weighed next to nothing, while offering all the advantages of ordinary granite ware. Other campers' comforts, too, had been secured, so that they even carried a certain amount of condensed food in the shape of milk powder; evaporated eggs that could be used to make excellent omelets in case of necessity; and even soup in double cans, with a layer of unslacked lime between, which, by the addition of a little water to the lime could be heated up beautifully without the aid of a fire.

[2] "In camp on the Big Sunflower."

When all of them started in to get busy, things quickly assumed a concentrated condition. Each article had its regular place where it would take up the least possible space. Why, by now every fellow had found out just how to do up his pack so that no sharp and uncomfortable edges would cut into his back; and when this condition has been reached, it means that the last word in packing has been learned.

Max himself saw to it that the fire was effectually "killed" before they quitted the scene of their night encampment. This he did by throwing water on the hissing embers until it was quite dead. If every party that spends a night in the wilderness took the same pains to put out their fire on leaving, many a magnificent stretch of timber would be spared from the ravages of a forest fire, that leaves only blackened tree trunks behind, and ruins thousands of acres of wooded land every year.

Although a fire may die down, and seem to have little life in it, there is no absolute surety unless water be used, that a rising wind may not fan the embers into renewed activity, until a dangerous spark is carried into some nest of dead leaves near by, and so the fire starts that man-power can seldom control.

"Three miles, he said, up this stream," observed Bandy-legs, as they started gaily forth, Max in the lead, and Toby bringing up the rear.

"And as no doubt the said stream meanders considerably in its course, that might mean only half the distance as the crow flies," remarked the leader, turning once more to look back toward the deserted camp, after the fashion of a carpenter who considers it wise to measure his post *once again* before applying the saw, because after the deed is done the parts can never be put together again; but everything seemed still, and not the faintest whisp of smoke crept lazily upward from the late camp-fire.

They walked along for a short distance, and then upon crossing a little rise, in order to skirt a bad section of marshy ground, it was discovered that they had a good chance to look backward. A rather pretty view rewarded their efforts, and as all the boys appreciated Nature in her fall dress, they stood for a minute drinking this in.

"You can follow the course of the stream for quite a distance, notice?" remarked Bandy-legs. "And I even see the place where we yanked Steve here out of that sand."

Steve frowned as he looked, and Max could see that he had gone a little white. The memory of his harrowed feelings on that occasion would stay with Steve for quite some time, and produce an unpleasant sensation every time it came before his mental vision.

Max also saw him shut his teeth very hard together, and was close enough to even catch a word or two the boy muttered savagely to himself.

"Never again!"

From that Max could judge the lesson had been impressed on Steve's mind indelibly; and that as long as he lived he would be careful how he entered an unknown stream when fishing; and especially how he became so engrossed in his sport as to stand a length of time in one spot, without working his feet up and down so as to make sure they were free from clinging sand.

They chatted from time to time as they proceeded, and of course all sorts of subjects cropped up to be discussed. Sometimes there was a little good-natured dispute concerning something or other, for boys have different minds, and are apt to view things from various angles; but as time passed they made such good progress that Max presently announced his belief they must presently glimpse the seven birch trees mentioned by Obed Grimes, as marking the place where they were to quit the bank of the stream.

At the time they stopped to look backward Max had scanned the country behind them, looking for some trace of another camp smoke, but seeing fond of "working his way," and often slipped out of things when he could manage it—some fellows always do get hold of the smaller end of the log that is being carried, as if by instinct; though it would be hardly fair to call them shirkers.

They rested for something like ten minutes. Then Max started up.

"Here's the trail Obed told us about," he observed, pointing down at his feet as though he had been looking about him while recuperating after that three mile carry. "And I guess we might as well be going on. For one I'm beginning to feel quite curious to see that lodge of his under the pines and hemlocks, as well as learn what he is doing with his fox farm."

Bandy-legs opened his mouth, and then considered it better not to voice the question he had on the tip of his tongue, for he shut his jaws tight together again, and did not speak; Max noticing this, it caused him to smile in quiet satisfaction. That was a very disagreeable habit of Bandy-legs, always questioning things, and wanting double proof before he would put the stamp of his approval on them; and Max kept hoping that in the process of time it could be broken up.

It was not difficult to follow the trail, even though at times this proved to be rather faint and undecided; at least it turned out to be an easy task with the four chums, simply because they were accustomed to such things. A greenhorn might have lost the track many times, and made a none. He had in mind the story told by Obed concerning the presence in the vicinity of another party, and his suspicions concerning their base intentions. Apparently Max must have believed what the woods boy said, even though he could see no sign of a camp that morning.

"I've got an idea the seven birches are just over yonder, boys!" announced Steve, who possessed good eyesight. "Twice now I've glimpsed something white among the thickets of undergrowth; and you can see that the creek is beginning to swing around so as to lead us in that direction."

"G-g-guess you're about r-r-right, Steve!" declared Toby Jucklin, instantly; "to t-t-tell you the t-t-truth, I've been squinting that same p-p-patch of white myself q-q-quite some little time now."

It turned out to be just as Steve had prophesied. They soon discovered a bunch of birches growing from the stump of a larger tree that had long ago fallen under the ax of a woodsman.

"There are seven, all right—count 'em!" announced Steve with a vein of exultation in his voice, just as though by right of discovery those birches really belonged to him.

"Let's call a little rest before we tackle the last round," begged Bandy-legs, as they arrived alongside the landmark mentioned by Obed; and without waiting for the others to assent he dropped his pack, and threw himself down on an especially inviting bit of moss, heaving a great sigh of relief; for be it known, Bandy-legs was not especially "mountain out of a mole-hill," as Steve aptly put it, when referring to the matter.

Soon they were casting eager glances ahead, under the impression that they must certainly be drawing near the object of their search. Even Bandy-legs had by now apparently arrived at the belief that Obed was "straight," and that he really did have some sort of home in this secluded region. The directions had turned out to be exact, from the three-mile tramp along the stream and the "seven birches, count 'em"; to the winding trail that led from that point deeper into the woods.

"Looky there, isn't that some sort of high wire fence?" demanded Steve, suddenly.

"And, say, I got a plain whiff of sweet hickory wood smoke then, believe me," added Bandy-legs, in some excitement, and evidently forgetting that not long before he had been skeptical regarding the existence of any lodge or fox farm.

"Well, there's the answer right before you," laughed Max; and as they stared in the direction their leader was pointing, the balance of the little party saw what seemed to be the "cutest" little cabin fashioned from sawn logs, and nestling in a happy fashion directly under the clustering pines and hemlocks, that hung over it most protectingly, as though with the intention of keeping the winter snows from weighing down the sloping roof.

At one end was a chimney made of slabs of wood, with the chinks filled in with mud that, in the process of time, aided by the heat of the fire, had become as hard as cement or adamant; and from this there curled wreaths of lazily ascending blue smoke, the source of that delightful odor that had drifted to Bandy-legs's nostrils.

CHAPTER VI

THE LODGE OF MANY WONDERS

"There's Obed right now, waving at us from the doorway of his cabin," announced Steve, even as they looked at the picture made by the little log structure nestling so cozily under the dark foliage of the resinous trees that never lost their green look, even when snow covered the mountains to the depth of several feet.

They hurried forward to join the owner of the woods lodge, who had evidently expected them to put in an appearance about this time of day, figuring just when they would break camp, and how long it would take them to make the "carry."

He shook hands with each of his new-found friends in turn, and warmly, too. Even Bandy-legs seemed to feel that his unworthy suspicions of the other could have no foundation, to judge from the hearty way in which he greeted Obed.

Max was quick to see that Obed looked pleased at their coming. He also wondered why the other seemed to raise his eyebrows now and then, and smile as though certain thoughts he entertained were quite amusing. But, then, seeing what a lonely life the young fur farmer must be leading, so far away from his kind, and wrapped up in his singular calling, after all, it was not so queer that he should act in this way, upon having visitors, and boys of his own age, in the bargain.

They were ushered inside the lodge, and here another surprise greeted them. Max in particular was astonished to find that the small building contained so much in the way of comforts. If he had thought of the matter at all, he probably expected to find just an ordinary shack, such as nine boys in ten would be contented with building, and that Obed was putting up with all sorts of discomforts.

The contrary proved to be the truth, for there were numerous things in sight to cause a visitor to express surprise. Why, Obed even used *aluminum cooking utensils* equal to theirs, though not meant for camping particularly; there were several rocking chairs, and one big fireside chair that looked mighty inviting indeed, as it flanked the broad hearth where Obed had a blaze going.

The kitchen lay at the back, and actually had a wood stove in it, capable of baking bread or biscuits on occasion. Water, too, had been piped to the cabin from some spring farther up the rise; though, in the dead of winter a supply must of necessity be obtained from some other source since this would be frozen up.

These things, and many others along the same line, caused Max to survey Obed with a new source of wonder. Who was this remarkable boy, and how on earth did he come to possess such a magical lodge up here in the unpeopled wilderness? Why, a rich man could hardly have surrounded himself with more in the way of comforts; and yet, according to his language, and his account of himself, Obed was only an ordinary child of the woods, one of the very numerous Grimes tribe, many of whom doubtless gained their living by serving as guides in season.

Max, after staring around him in due wonder and admiration, turned again to Obed. He could see that the other was observing them with that merry twinkle in his eyes? and evidently expecting his guests to express amazement at finding so wonderful a habitation where they had anticipated so little.

"Its just splendid, that's the only word I can find to express my feelings, Obed," Max hastened to say, at which the other laughed aloud.

"Course, now, you-all are awonderin' jest how a poor woods boy like me 'd ever git hold o' such a clever cabin," he went on to say; "but shucks! that's an easy one to explain. Yuh see, it was built by a man who had plenty o' money and poor health. He thought he could get well by stayin' here, and so he fixed her up to beat the band. That big chair he loved to sit in when the fire was agoin'. But jest as he got fixed so nice his wife sent for him to come back home; and, say, he had to go. So, havin' no use for his place here, he turned it over tuh me for a song, I c'n show yuh the bill o' sale. Yuh see, I got to know Mr. Coombs right well, for he was interested in my ijee o' startin' a fur farm. Well, he's dead now. I often think when I'm sittin' here enjoyin' what he built that somehow his spirit must be a hoverin' around, cause he certainly *did* love this place a heap."

The explanation entirely satisfied Max, though of course that skeptic of a Bandy-legs had to let his eyebrows go up in an arch as he listened; but then Bandy-legs would doubt anything that savored of the uncommon. Max simply frowned at him and paid no more attention to his manner.

"You were certainly mighty lucky to fall heir to such a lovely little home as this, Obed," Steve was saying, with a streak of envy in his voice. "Say, I'd just be tickled half to death now if I could spend a month up here with you. There must be plenty of game around, I reckon; and it'd be a real delight to keep house in a little palace like this. But how are you going to tuck us away for the night, Obed, if I might be so bold as to ask, seeing that as yet we haven't had an invite to stay over?"

"Oh! that's easily managed," replied the other, with, another of his queer laughs. "You haven't begun to see all the wonders o' this lodge. Mr. Coombs amused himself for a whole summer havin' it built. He put a heap o' his own ijees into the same, too. Yuh see, he used to be a sea captain once on a time, and that gave him the notion to have tables that folded against the wall so as tuh take mighty little room. Then seem' as how he might expect to have company some time or other, look how he fixed the bunks along the walls."

With that Obed turned a button that none of them had thus far noticed, fastened on the wall Immediately a section slipped down exposing a cavity beyond that proved to be a regular sleeping bunk, fully capable of "housing" any ordinary person. It was plain to be seen that his sea education had given Mr. Coombs the idea carried out in this remarkable fashion.

"Beats anything I ever struck!" admitted the admiring Steve, as he pushed forward to peep inside the cavity that seemed to offer such a comfortable bed.

"But hardly big enough for the whole bunch of us, I'm afraid, Obed," urged Bandy-legs, with the idea, of course, of drawing the other out.

"This is one bunk," said Obed, calmly, "there are three jest like it along the two walls, makin' four in all. So yuh see it's jest like Mr. Coombs, he figgered on my having you-all stop over with me some fine day. Then I c'n make up a bed on that 'ere couch, which is softer 'n any o' the bunks. *He* used to sleep, on it all the time, did Mr. Coombs."

"Well, I must say this is a revelation to me," admitted Max, his face showing how pleased he felt. "And you were lucky, as Steve here just said, to fall in with such a fine man as Mr. Coombs, at the time you started your fur farm. I suppose it was the interest he took in it that made him hand over this cabin, when he learned that his plans for staying here could never be carried out."

"Why, yes, mostly that," agreed Obed, turning a little red. "P'raps I ought to tell yuh that I chanced to do Mr. Coombs a little favor when we first met. Yuh see, I happened to come on him in the woods. He'd started out to find a certain kind o' sapling that he wanted right bad to use; and not bein' used to findin' his way around, he jest naturally got lost. But that wasn't the wust o' it. In using his ax to chop down a sapling he kim across, what did he do but cut his foot, and it was bleeding like fun when I ketched his shouts, and kim up. Course, I soon fixed that foot, and since he was only a little dried-up speck o' a man I managed to tote him on my back most ways home here. He chose to think I'd done him a *great* favor, and after that he was always sayin' he meant to repay me some day. Well, he certainly did when he turns over this here neat contraption at a price that was dirt cheap, and which I'd be ashamed to mention to yuh. That's how it come I got this cabin."

How simple the explanation was after all, and how Bandy-legs must feel his cheeks burn with shame at the thought of having suspected this same Obed of trying to deceive them. Max could easily picture the ex-sea captain seated in that capacious fireside chair with the tufted cushion, and perhaps smoking his long-stemmed pipe with the air of a man who believed he had found what he had long sought, peace and comfort combined, only to have a summons come that he dared not disobey.

"Make yourselves to hum," said Obed, cheerily. "Here, drop the packs over in this corner. If later on so be yuh want to git anything out o' the same it'll be easy done. And seein' as I've got dinner started, I guess we wont take a turn around the farm till it's been stowed away."

Although, of course, all of the boys were eager to see what a fur farm looked like, where those wonderful black foxes that brought such, a big price in the London markets were being bred in captivity, none of them objected to sitting down and taking a rest. Bandy-legs and Steve in particular made a bolt for the big chair, though the latter was too quick for his competitor, and managed to ensconce himself within its capacious embrace before Bandy-legs arrived.

"Start earlier next time, Bandy-legs!" crowed the proud possessor of the coveted seat, as he spread himself so as to occupy it all. "But after I've tried it out I'll vacate, because I expect to get busy in that bully little kitchen, and help friend Obed sling the grub for dinner."

So Bandy-legs had to content himself with a seat on the couch. He might have been observed sniffing the air with avidity, however, as though he had caught some enticing odor stealing out of the oven of the cook stove, that was not unlike fresh bread being well browned; and there was nothing Bandy-legs loved better than the crust part of a fresh baking—he always had a compact with the cook at home to save him the "run-over" portions, which he looked upon as a prize well worth having.

Soon Obed left them there in the larger room and vanished within the kitchen. It was a challenge to Steve which he could not long resist. Bandy-legs kept watching him glance toward the connecting doors. His whole manner was that of a boy who, although making no sound, might be "sicking" one dog on another. No sooner had Steve left the capacious fireside chair than Bandy-legs slipped into it; and after that he was not meaning' to be dislodged until the summons came to gather about the table to discuss the midday meal. Bandy-legs liked eating as well as the next one; but he loved his ease more, and was well content to have some other fellow do the hard work of getting the meal ready; his time would come when he had to "work his jaws" in disposing of his portion of the spread.

The more Max looked about him the greater his wonder became. All manner of thoughts surged through that active mind of his. He had already conceived the greatest sort of secret admiration for the extraordinary woods boy, even before he had glimpsed that remarkable fur farm which the other was successfully running. Plainly, then, this same Obed Grimes was bound to be a credit to his family; and all those people bearing the strange names given by Obed would some day find cause to feel proud of having such an enterprising relative.

Obed proved to be a pretty good cook, despite the humility with which he had remarked that of course he could not expect to compete on even terms with fellows who had had so many better opportunities to acquire the "knack" of things, than had come his way.

The bread was as fine as any Bandy-legs had ever eaten in his own home, where a high-priced cook held sway over the kitchen. There was also a meat pie that seemed delicious, both as to crust and contents, when opened; though Obed in-formed them that it was made of canned beef, and even displayed the recent tin jacket, with its telltale label, as confirmation to his assertion.

"Yuh see, boys," he remarked, laughingly, "I don't want yuh to think I'd poach a deer in the close season, and palm it off as mountain mutton, like they do at some o' the big hotels up here in the Adirondacks, I'm told. Course I do shoot a deer once in a while in season; and lots o' pa'tridges, they bein' so tame yuh c'n knock them over as they sit on the lower limb o' a tree after flushin'. I ketch wheens o' trout, too, from time to time; but I give yuh my word I never yet killed anything when the law was on it, never!"

When Obed said a thing in his emphatic way, he was to be relied on, Max thought. The woods boy could look very sober at times, though, as a rule, there was that merry gleam in his eye that told how much he loved a joke.

Altogether they had a delightful meal, and what was even better, there was an abundance to give every one three bountiful helpings, which fact pleased Bandy-legs and Steve in particular. The former, on passing his plate—for they actually had such articles at this wonderful lodge under the pines—for the third help, excused himself by remarking aside:

"It's queer what a *terrible* appetite toting a pack a few miles over a carry gives a fellow. Now, at home I'm generally satisfied with one portion, but once let me get into the harness, and I seem to have no end of *capacity*. Say, I'd eat you out of house and home, Obed, if I stayed very long at your ranch."

"No danger o' that, I guess, Bandy-legs," replied the other, for he had of course taken quite naturally to calling these new friends by their customary names, just as boys always do get on quick terms of familiarity. "Last time I went to town I laid in quite a wheen o' stuff. Then there's always the crick to git trout outen; and in a short time you could shoot pa'tridges without breakin' the game laws. So don't let that worry yuh any. I'm on'y too tickled to have some fellers around. It does git kinder lonely here, sometimes, I own up."

"Whew! I should think it would, Obed," said Steve, lost in admiration for the amazing nerve displayed by the woods boy in remaining all by himself, winter and summer, seldom, if ever, seeing a human face, and apparently devoting all his energies to making his fur farm experiment turn out to be a success. "Nothing would tempt me to stick it out here a whole winter. Why, I'd die of the blues, and let the black foxes go to the dickens, while I made break for the nearest town, so I could hear the sound of a human voice."

Obed looked at him gravely, and heaved a sigh.

"Yep, I feels that ways, too, sometimes, Steve," he said presently; "and let me tell yuh the temptation is nigh more'n I c'n stand; but I jest shuts my teeth together, and tells myself that I started in to do this job, and I'm agoin' to stick it out or know the reason why. Then I git my second wind agin' and it's all right. Once I used to give in right easy, but I'm broke now o' that bad habit, I guess."

CHAPTER VII

THE YOUNG MAGICIAN

The more Max listened to Obed talk on the one subject that seemed to be his pet hobby, that of raising valuable fur-bearing animals for the market, the deeper grew his conviction that the woods boy was well worth studying.

He might talk after the manner of an uneducated boy, but Max knew that this could not be the case. Even though the main lot of numerous "Grimeses" were following the humble occupation of guides amidst the extensive stretches of the Adirondacks, and possibly many of them would be found to be boors, save along the line of woodcraft, Obed had managed to pick up considerable knowledge, somehow or other.

When trying to explain how this idea of successfully raising "silver" black foxes took such a main grip on his imagination, he brought out a batch of clippings which he had managed to get hold of in some manner, Max could not even guess how.

Some of these were fantastic in their revelations, while others were authentic interviews with parties who for years had been secretly engaged in the business of fur farming. This was away up on Prince Edward Island beyond Nova Scotia, said to be the place best situated geographically for the purpose, as these animals require a severe climate in order that their pelt assumes its richest and heaviest crop. A black fox farm started down in Florida would not produce furs worth offering for sale.

Max was intensely interested with one account in particular connected with the extensive pioneer silver fox ranch. He even asked the privilege of copying the same for future reference, because he knew that statements he might make later on would be skeptically received by many people who had never dreamed that any species of furs were so valuable that young pups could be worth more than their weight in gold.

That the boy reader of this story may also stock up with information that will better enable him to understand what enterprising Obed Grimes was trying to do on a small scale, I am tempted to give the main items in this newspaper article, every word of which is said to be literally true.

Since this account was first printed some years ago, other farms along similar lines have been started away up near Calgary, in the Canadian Province of Alberta, and are said to be doing excellently, one ranch near Midnapore reporting a start with twelve pair, and the pack now counting thirty-seven in all.

But here is the main part of the clipping, well worth reading:

There is something novel about a ranch which consists of spaces covering 150 feet of ground. Chappell, now president of the Sydney Chamber of Commerce, Nova Scotia, owns seventy pairs of silver black foxes, and his ranch is split up into small inclosures of that size, covered with wire on four sides, the wire being buried four feet under ground, attached to a concrete base, and turned in several feet. The silver black fox tries to root its way to freedom, and this is the way the breeder prevents his escape.

When the foxes mate we also mate a pair of black cats of the ordinary domestic variety. As soon as the young are born, we take the fox pups away from the mother fox, and the kittens away from the mother cat, and make the cat foster-mother to the fox cubs. In this way we are able to rear a more domesticated breed of foxes.

For twenty years this business of raising foxes of the silver black species was really kept under cover, because of its great possibilities for making big money. With the last four or five years the business has become organized, and today many millions of dollars are invested in it.

The last lot of animals slaughtered was in 1910. There were forty-three pelts sent to London at that time. They brought as high as $3,800, the average fetching $1,500. Silver black fox is the rarest fur utilized by man. The Russian sable, otter, and South Sea seal are practically eliminated for commercial purposes, due to international laws which prohibit the killing of these animals for the next ten or fifteen years, so as to give them a chance to increase.

Only 800 pairs of live foxes were placed on sale last year. Fewer than 50 of that number were killed and their fur sold. The rest went for breeding purposes, because fur farms are starting up in many favorable places. The men who raise silver foxes on Prince Edward Island know the game. They started in it as boys many years ago.

"In the provinces of Prince Edward, Nova Scotia, and New Brunswick, men and women interested in breeding foxes have been made wealthy. They were poor people ten years ago. Today they live in town houses, own their own automobiles, and yet continue to give the strictest attention to all the details connected with their singular farming industry."

Obed was extremely modest in what he told concerning his own small beginning. Max, having also read in one of the clippings that a pair of gilt-edged silver black foxes were worth all the way up to $30,000, was, of course, doubly curious to learn whether those with which Obed started could be the genuine article, and if so, how had he managed to obtain them.

It seemed to be only a game in which rich persons could enter. Obed understood just what must be passing in the mind of the other, and at the first opportunity he hastened to explain.

"I was just chock full o' this business," he went on to say, "when I ran across Mr. Coombs. Yuh remember I told yuh about how that came about, and that he seemed to think I'd saved his life." Well, he and me kept house together here for some months, and then one day thar come the biggest surprise I ever had. He fetched a crate along up from town in a wagon he hired; and say, inside the same was the finest pair o' silver blacks I ever saw. Then some more wagons begun to show up fetchin' rolls of wire netting, and bags o' cement to make concrete with. Mr. Coombs had gone into the fur raisin' business for keeps, and I was to have an interest in the game. He had an agreement all written out that both o' us signed before a justice, which fixed things up. Half the proceeds o' the fur farm was to come to me, while I stayed here to look after things.

"Well, sir, we worked like fun to git the stockade built 'cording to form; and our mated pair o' foxes planted in the same. Since then I've fixed three more enclosures, ready for an increase o' stock. Mr. Coombs, he called this the Lone Lodge Black Fox Farm, and I guess the name will stick even after I get to selling off some o' the product."

It was simply wonderful, all of the eager listeners thought. Max could hardly believe his ears, and yet so far as he could make out Obed seemed in dead earnest. Besides, he had the documents to prove the truth of his story, he said, which he would spread before them a little later on.

As for that skeptic, Bandy-legs, he rolled his eyes up many times while listening, and seemed to be swallowing it with considerable difficulty. Toby and Steve never questioned the veracity of the narrator; they were simply amazed at the immensity of the enterprise that had sprung up almost like a mushroom, over night. Millions on millions of dollars invested in artificial fur farming, and the general public utterly in the dark concerning the facts until recently, when its scope could no longer be concealed, like a light hidden under a bushel.

"And now that you've kinder got an idea of what a big fur farm might be like," the singular woods boy went on to say, rising as he spoke, "s'pose yuh meander out and take a look at my humble beginnin'. I surely hope yuh won't run down my efforts, 'cause o' course things ain't got to runnin' full swing yet. But the cubs are nigh big enough to be taken to market."

"How many have you got, Obed?" asked Max, following the other out of the cabin.

"One pair nearly grown, and another just two months old. I've been mighty lucky in not losing a single pup so far," came the reply over Obed's shoulder; and he might be pardoned for putting just a mite of pride in his tones, for he had accomplished something worth while for a new beginner at the business.

"But if you expect to keep in this line," said Bandy-legs quickly, as though he voiced a suspicion that kept cropping up in his mind, "why do you want to dispose of that first pair of pups?"

Obed laughed good-naturedly.

"I'll tell yuh, Bandy-legs," he said, confidentially. "In the first place breeders like to change their stock, so as to bring new blood into the pens. Then again, why, I happens to need the money that's comin' to me for my share. A fellow has got to live up here in the mountains, and grub costs a wheen o' hard cash, 'specially when yuh got a good appetite, which seems to fit me all right. But if I get what I'm hopin' for it'll be all right, and I reckons thar'll come some years before we let more foxes get away from this same farm."

So he took them to where he had his main enclosure, in which the boys found the parent foxes. They may have become somewhat accustomed to seeing Obed, and hearing the sound of his coaxing voice, for even the most timid of wild animals in the process of time comes to recognize the one who supplies their wants along the line of daily food. But possibly Bandy-legs or Steve chanced to laugh, or speak out loud, for the old foxes took the alarm; and it was only after constant efforts on the part of Obed, with his familiar call to dinner, that caused them to show themselves at all.

They were certainly beauties. Max wondered more than ever at the nerve of Obed in trying to start a silver black fox farm in this section, with no one save himself apparently in charge. He feared that the enterprise would be doomed to certain disaster. The smart woods boy might be successful in raising a crop of valuable youngsters in the fox line; but sooner or later some unscrupulous men, guides out of a job perhaps, and loaded with strong drink, would try to make a secret raid on his preserves, and clean him out in a single night. Fox pelts worth thousands of dollars must tempt some men beyond their fears, or power of resistance.

Max made up his mind he would talk about this with Obed before he left. He wondered at the short-sighted policy of the executor of Mr. Coombs' estate in allowing so much money to be tied up in this property without proper safeguards. If it was intended to continue the fox farm now that it gave all evidences of possible success surely the boy should have an assistant, some strong woodsman who could by his presence and readiness to do battle awe any intended transgressors.

They next visited the enclosure where the two pair of little foxes played and slept and ate their fill, daily increasing in size and value. They were also timid, though in due time Obed managed to get them to show themselves; for hunger is a powerful inducement, and the smell of favorite food a lure difficult to resist.

"Of course," explained the young fur farmer, while they were watching the inmates of the second enclosure, "I don't have black cats up here yet to carry out them directions exactly; but I'm aiming to do that also pretty soon. Yep, and after this set o' pups has been sold, if they fetch all I count on, I'm goin' to have a talk with the lawyer that looks after Mr. Coombs' estate. He promised to come up and see what could be done about extendin' the farm. And then I guess it's goin' to be time to hire a helper, seein' I can't do everything by myself."

"That was just what I meant to speak to you about, Obed!" exclaimed Max. "You oughtn't to try to stay here another winter all by yourself. Besides, some unscrupulous men might raid your enclosures while you were off hunting, or fishing, and break up your business. It isn't safe, Obed; and I know from what you said before about suspecting strangers were around here right now, that you're getting anxious yourself."

The boy drew a long breath, and nodded his head. Into his eyes crept a look quite the opposite of that merry gleam usually nestling there. Yes, plainly Obed *was* worried over something; and Max believed he had put his finger directly on the sore spot when he spoke of a possible raid on the fur product of the singular farm.

"Can you find just such a reliable man as you want, Obed?" asked Steve.

"That part ain't so hard," he was told. "Fact is I've got him more'n half engaged a'ready. His name is Jerry Stocks, and he's a woods guide. Been a heap interested in this game ever since we started up. Fact is, Jerry has done a heap o' things for me from time to time, 'cause yuh see I couldn't work it all. He lives 'bout 'leven miles off that ways. We've fixed a way to signal to each other by flyin' a little white flag from two low peaks. When I want Jerry I run my flag up, and if he's home, why the next day, or mebbe sooner, he shows up. But shucks! that wouldn't keep me from losin' my stock if there was a real raid."

He went on talking further, and the boys picked up considerable more valuable information, for Obed was apparently well posted on the subject, which had occupied his thoughts night and day.

So he told them that perhaps, if all went well, he might take up a companion industry, being nothing more nor less than trying to raise mink or otter in captivity.

"'Course I know it isn't done to any great extent yet," he explained, "but that's no reason there shouldn't be some ready money picked up in the business. It wouldn't pay anything like the foxes, and for that reason I'd go slow about it. Oh! I've got a heap o' ways for gettin' the ready cash to keep up my share o' the expenses o' the farm here. I've found two bee trees, and sent the honey to market too. Got nigh twenty dollars for the honey. Then I dig ginseng roots times when there's nothing else to do. Come over with me and see my frog pond. Last shipment o' big fat saddles brought me a neat little wad o' money, and they don't cost me a cent, if yuh want to know it."

The four boys looked at each other in increased wonderment. What manner of chap was this same Obed, to be able to wrest a living from a bounteous Nature in the clever way he did? Steve in particular was loud in his praise.

"Why, Obed, old fellow," he burst out with, "you're just the same kind of an enterprising chap Max here has always been. Why, it was his grand idea about there being mussels aplenty in the Big Sunflower down our way that started us into making a try for fresh-water pearls in the river. We found 'em, too, some thousands of dollars' worth, of them; and when the news leaked out, whee! the farmers, all around, had a tough time getting their harvests home, because every hand was treading for mussels in the creeks and small rivers for thirty miles around Carson. Why, I bet you it'd be as hard to find a fresh-water clam down our way now as a needle in a haystack; they're all cleaned out. You see, Max here had read about pearls being found out in Indiana and other places, and that gave him the big idea; just like you got set on the fur farm business by reading about it."

They duly inspected the marsh where Obed hunted his big greenback frogs when he thought the crop warranted a thinning out.

"They're always in demand down New York ways, whar they fetch a dollar a pound for the saddles," he explained; "and let me tell yuh it doesn't take a great many o' them to weigh that much. I've got some granddaddy bouncers here that'd make you stare to see 'em; but they don't show up much at this time o' day."

"And how do you get them by the wholesale when you want to market any?" asked Steve. "I've shot many a one with a small Flobert rifle; or else caught them with a piece of red flannel fixed on a small hook, attached by a short cord to a stout pole."

"Well, men in the regular frog-raising business couldn't go about it as slow as that," said the other, "though I have shot a few o' the big uns that way, 'cause they was too tricky to be grabbed with my hand net. If you stay with me a spell we'll get more'n one mess o' frog legs, if yuh likes them."

Bandy-legs was seen to work his lips as though his month fairly watered at the pleasing prospect; for those who are fond of the dish say that frogs' legs are more delicate than the best spring chicken, with just a little taste of fish about them that rather adds to the piquancy.

Having by this time exhausted about all the sights of the wonderful farm the boys headed back again toward the cabin. Max could not but notice that Obed showed signs of uneasiness while away, and cast frequent glances in the direction where under those whispering pines and the dark green hemlocks his lone lodge stood.

Therefore Max was not very much surprised when, as he and Obed strolled along in the rear of the other three, who were chatting, and arguing about certain matters, the young fur farmer pressed his arm confidentially, and went on to say:

"I'd like to tell yuh something, Max, 'cause I own up it's gettin' on my nerves. I thought nothin' could bother me any, but now that the time is so close at hand when I mean tuh sell that pair o' grown pups, and get the money I need so bad, why, things look kinder different. Fact is, Max," he went on, allowing his voice to sink into a mysterious stage whisper, "somebody was lookin' around in my cabin while I was down at your camp last evenin'. I know this because things was more or less upset; and I reckon my comin' back scared the man away, whoever he may have been!"

CHAPTER VIII

PRODUCTS OF THE FUR FARM

"That looks bad, Obed," Max hastened to say, feeling a perceptible thrill at the very thought of being on hand to assist this enterprising boy defend his property, which he had made so valuable, through his own efforts in most part. "I saw a smoke last evening, too, which must have been made by a camp-fire. I wondered if there were deer hunters up here so early; or if some men might be after your foxes. Of course that idea only came to me after you had told us about your enterprise, and how valuable the pelts were."

"It's mighty tough," avowed Obed, between his set teeth, "to be so nigh success, and then face failure. I've been tempted to signal for Jerry to come over and help me stand guard a spell. Yuh see, I ought to be on my way to town with that pair o' nearly-grown young blacks. I know whar I c'n get more for 'em alive than for their pelts if I took the time to cure the same, which I don't want to do. Oh! I've just *got* to sell 'em, and that's all thar is about it. I've dreamed about the day I'd get that check, and show—er, that lawyer managin' Mr. Coombs' estate that all I told him was true. Once I have the proof that thar's big money in raisin' silver blacks, he's promised to do anything in reason I ask."

Max made up his mind on the spot.

"Look here, Obed," was the way he talked, for Max always believed that it was good policy to "hit the nail directly on the head;" especially when the subject was of considerable importance, "what's to hinder you going off with that pair of live blacks, and disposing of them, while the four of us stay here and run your fur farm for you? It would only take a few days, and we've got the time to spare. Of course you'd have to trust us to the limit, to leave things in our charge; but we'd surely be pleased to help you out. And depend on it, nobody would steal any of the other inmates of the pens while we were on deck. We've got only one gun along, but that is a repeating Marlin, always to be depended on to do its work."

The woods boy was visibly affected by hearing Max say this. He reached for the other's hand and squeezed it almost fiercely.

"Oh! it's kind of you to say that, Max!" he exclaimed, as though the words sprang directly from his heart. "And d'ye know I'm tempted to take you at your word. For I *must* get those pups delivered as I promised. Everything depends on that deal. The man saw them three months ago, and we made a bargain. I was to deliver the pups to him by the time first snow flew; and it's due any day now, you know."

A singular thing had happened, and Max, while deeply interested in what Obed was saying, could not help but notice that for once the woods boy had spoken without a sign of the rude dialect which up to then had marked his manner of speech. This further aroused the curiosity of Max, who to himself was saying:

"I hit the mark when I guessed Obed was smarter than he let on, and could talk just as well as the next fellow when he chose. He's just fallen into speaking that way through his association with these rough people up here, his own folks likely enough. Or else he likes to pull the wool over our eyes, just for a joke."

Aloud Max continued to reassure the other.

"Then consider it as good as settled, Obed," he said, "that we'll hang around here a short while. If you think best you can get that Jerry to come over, and keep his finger on the pulse. Perhaps it might be wise, too, because he'd know just what to do in case there was any trouble among the foxes left in the pens; and it is all new to us, remember."

"Yuh've relieved my mind a heap, Max, sure yuh have," Obed told him, again relapsing into the vernacular that is usually a part of a woods guide's language. "And tonight I'll set the traps I've got fixed.

Mebbe if so be trespassers come a skulkin' around they might git a little surprise. But I'll show yuh what I'm mentionin' later on. Jest now I on'y want to tell yuh I'm mighty glad I dropped into yer camp last evenin' 'stead o' slippin' away, like I fust thought o' doin'."

"But you don't want me to look on this matter as a secret, do you, Obed?"

The other started, Max thought, and looked quickly at him.

"Now what might yuh be meanin' by that, Max?" he presently asked, a bit anxiously.

"Oh! I only wanted to have your permission to tell my three chums what you've been saying to me," explained Max. "Of course I know what their answer will be when I put it up to them. We've really come here on what Bandy-legs calls a wild goose hunt, for there isn't one chance in ten that we'll ever be able to find Roland Chase; so our time is really pretty much our own, to do with as we will. And Obed, all of us have taken such a big interest in your enterprise up here, that we'll be only too happy to lend you a helping hand. You are so near success now that it'd be a shame if you fell down through no fault of your own."

"That's what I keep tellin' myself too, Max, don't you know!" exclaimed the now excited Obed. "I've hugged that hope close to my heart month after month, and now when I c'n almost whiff the success I've prayed for it'd nearly kill me to lose everything. Oh! I jest wants a couple of weeks at the most, and then I'll show 'em, yes, I will. They all said I'd make a dead failure out o' my fur farm; but yuh c'n see it's comin' along right smart."

When they reached the cabin the boys threw themselves down on the soft yielding turf near-by to "loaf" as Bandy-legs properly expressed it; and surely he could do this as well as any boy who ever drew breath.

Max took occasion to tell the others what he and Obed had been talking about. All of them were deeply interested. They looked angrily at each other when Max explained how the woods boy had found traces of some intruder who had actually entered his lone cabin while he, Obed, was away in their company; also telling how the other strongly suspected that a dastardly plot had been hatched, looking to the robbing of the pens connected with the silver fox fur farm.

Obed was inside doing something at the time, and so Max felt that he could talk freely. He meant that his three chums should know everything in the beginning, before he called on them to decide whether they would stay over a few days, and guard the property, while Obed was marketing his first proceeds in a distant city; for the pups were really too valuable to be trusted to the tender mercies of an express company, Obed thought.

"I don't exactly understand how Obed knows that there *is* a conspiracy hatched up against him, to complete the ruination of his enterprise," continued Max; "but he seems to think some party has a deep grudge against him. It may be we'll know more about this later on; but for the present I've promised Obed I'd put up a proposition to you."

"Then let's hear it, Max!" exclaimed Touch-and-Go Steve, "though I reckon we c'n all give a pretty close guess at what's coming."

"Why, Obed wants to get away with that pair of grown pups, so he can deliver them to the man he's bargained with; and I've proposed that we stay here a few days, and guard his property while he's off. Is there any objection to that plan? I told him I expected I could count on my chums to stick by me."

"I should say you could, Max," chuckled Bandy-legs. "Why, I'm fairly counting on depopulating that big frog marsh while we're hanging around this section. And say, Steve here could keep us supplied with trout galore, if only he fished from the bank, and didn't wade in."

Both the others were equally prompt to agree. Indeed Toby "fell all over himself," as Steve termed it, in his eagerness to give assent; and could only recover after coming to an abrupt halt, taking one of his customary big breaths, and then giving a sharp whistle, after which he finished what he was saying as nicely as anything.

And that settled it, just as Max had been confident would be the case; for he knew his chums too well to believe they would be willing to let such a brave fight be lost when the goal seemed so near. Obed Grimes had proved to be a fellow after their own hearts, and they found themselves deeply interested in his fortunes.

So when the woods boy came out again—Max suspected that he had purposely withdrawn from the scene in order not to embarrass them while making their decision—he was told how they all felt. And Obed went around shaking hands, with the tears in his eyes. Plainly he had his whole heart wrapped up in the successful outcome of this odd venture; and when the clouds began to loom up overhead this proffered assistance on the part of the four chums was gratefully received.

"This is mighty nice o' yuh, boys," he kept telling them, as though really at a loss for appropriate words best calculated to express the state of his feelings; "and I ain't goin' to ever forget it, either. Now I feel that I c'n start out right away, the day after tomorrow, and deliver them pups to Mr. Sheckard. Say, mebbe I won't be a proud boy when he hands me that big check, and I know that I've won out against all odds!"

His eyes glowed at the very thought, and Max was more than glad he and his comrades had the chance to render so resolute a chap slight assistance. For it would really be a pleasure for them to stay there at that wonderful little lodge under the whispering pines, and keep house while Obed was away. Then, too, Jerry would be on hand, ready with his advice and knowledge, so as to do the proper thing. As to any rash prowler stealing the valuable foxes, day or night, well, they would see to it a constant watch was kept, and that the gun was always ready to block any nasty little game like that.

Later on, Max amused himself lolling in Mr. Coombs' big fireside chair, which he had moved near one of the windows. He had run across a number of books on a shelf, and was engaged in looking them over, though hardly bothering to actually read. Nevertheless, he seemed to be quite curious concerning them, and when Obed chanced to come in, Max naturally asked concerning the volumes.

"Oh! yuh see, some o' them belong to me," the woods boy remarked, without hesitation, "and t'others they were left here by Mr. Coombs. He was a great reader; and besides, he'd traveled all over the known world. Yuh remember I said he was a sea captain, and that he made his fortune carryin' cargoes from the Far East to England and America. Sometime I'll tell yuh a few of the queer adventures he had in foreign countries. They've got lots o' thrills about 'em, too."

"Just so," ventured Max, casually, "and I once heard some people talking about a Mr. Coombs who had been a great traveler. Now I wonder if it could have been the same party. Was his first name Robert?"

"Oh! no, *my* Mr. Coombs' name was Jared," replied the other, promptly.

"Then, of course, it could not have been the same," added Max, smiling as though he had attained the object of his questioning; "but the similarity in names, and the fact that both men had traveled considerably, made me think it might, be so."

He once more dipped into the book he was holding, although watching Obed slily over the top of the volume. And when the woods boy had passed outside again, Max Hastings might have been seen to hurriedly turn back to the blank pages at the front of the book, scan several initials that were plainly written there, and then nod his head mysteriously, with a smile that gradually crept across his whole face; just as though something pleased him, which, for the time being, he chose to keep to himself.

CHAPTER IX

LAYING PLANS TO HELP OBED

It was only natural that Steve, always headstrong and impulsive, should be eager to find out what kind of plan might be arranged looking to keeping watch and ward over the fur farm during the nights to come. He had been impressed with the signs of anxiety which Obed plainly betrayed, when speaking of his belief concerning some sort of plot being hatched up against his peace of mind, and which would bring about the ultimate ruination of his unique and intensely interesting undertaking.

To Steve, the idea of a miserable rascal sneaking up in the night to destroy all that poor hardworking Obed had built up after many moons, was simply terrible. The more he considered it the greater became his secret anger; and of course this meant that his liking for the boy fur farmer grew in proportion.

During the afternoon, as the shadows began to lengthen perceptibly, Steve found occasion to broach the subject to his three chums. Max had come out of the cabin; evidently he had tired of looking over the books, which might do very well to pass away a long evening, or a rainy day when time dragged, but could not chain him down long when the sun was shining, the breeze rustling through the many-colored leaves still on the trees, and with all Nature beckoning.

So Steve crooked his finger toward Bandy-legs and Toby, lounging near by; and being in a humor themselves for any sort of thing, the pair hastened to join him. And Max, upon being pounced upon by the balance of the crowd, looked askance, knowing that something was in the wind.

"Strikes me, fellows," commenced Steve, "that We ought to be figuring on what we expect to do tonight."

"Huh! as for me," quickly responded Bandy-legs, "I'm expecting to do my share about slingin' together a dandy spread, with some of the fine grub we fetched along. This mountain air is something terrible when it comes to toning up *jaded appetites*. I feel as if I had a vacuum down about my middle all the time. I'm beginning to be alarmed about my condition. If it keeps on it's going to mean bankruptcy for my folks, that's all."

"About me, now," added Toby Jucklin, briskly, "I'm hoping to g-g-get a b-b-bully g-g-good sleep tonight; unless Max fixes it so we have to t-t-take t-t-turns standing sentry duty."

Steve looked disgusted.

"Oh! rats! I didn't mean anything like that, and you both know it," he told the two grinning chums. "What I was referring to was on the point of duty. We've agreed to stand back of our new friend, Obed, and see to it that he isn't robbed of the proceeds of his industry by unscrupulous scoundrels; and we've got to make good!"

"Hear! hear!" ejaculated Toby, pretending to clap his hands in applause.

"Steve, you're exhausting all the big words in the dictionary, with your high-flown language," warned Bandy-legs in mock severity. "But I get your meaning, all the same, and I also agree with your noble sentiments. Sure we're expecting to stand up for Obed and his pets; and we're likewise intending to make it hot for any old terrapin who comes creeping around here with the idea of making way with the wearers of that expensive fur. How about it, Max?"

"That's a settled thing," readily replied the one appealed to, and whose opinion, it was plain to be seen, would swing things one way or another, since the other fellows were in the habit of looking up to Max as their leader. "We can fix it up in regular orthodox style, each fellow having two hours on duty, and the rest of the night for sleep. Does that strike you as about right?"

"Well," remarked Steve, proudly, "it won't be the first occasion when this bunch has had to stand guard, not by a long sight. I can look back and see many a night when we had to keep an anchor to windward, or else lose something we prized a heap. Ever since we dug up all those mussels in the Big Sunflower, and found dandy pearls inside some of them, it seems to me we've had occasion from time to time to be envied by other people, and had to keep watch so we wouldn't be robbed. Oh! standing sentry is an old trick with us!"

"For my p-p-part," remarked Toby, yawning as he spoke, "I'd much rather think up some g-g-good s-s-scheme that would ease the s-s-strain, and allow us to s-s-sleep through the entire night."

"Please explain what you mean by saying that, Toby," demanded Steve; "you do get off the most mysterious communications sometimes, and muddle us all up."

"But there isn't anything q-q-queer about this, Steve," protested Toby. "All of you know I've been a g-g-great h-h-hand to make m-m-machinery take the place of h-h-hand power. What's the need of our s-s-staying awake p-p-part of the night, even, if by cudgeling our brains we c-c-could think up some g-g-good s-s-scheme that would answer the same purpose?"

"I can see *you* cudgeling your poor brains, all right, Toby," sneered Steve, who apparently did not take a great deal of stock in the other's ability for conceiving clever ideas: "and a pretty mess you'd make of it, in the bargain. Take it from me, they're cudgeled enough as it is."

"That will do for you, Steve," said Max. "I understand just what Toby means, and it's along the right line too. This is the age of progress, and up-to-date people don't want to depend on the old-time methods that were good enough for their grandfathers. Toby thinks one of us might suggest a scheme whereby we could guard the fox farm, and at the same time obtain our full quota of sleep. In other words, rig up a dummy to stand our trick as sentry. Isn't that it, Toby?"

"J-j-just what I had in my mind, Max," snapped Toby; "and any silly c-c-could easy see that."

"Sure, and the wise ones had to be told," chirped Steve, jauntily. "But never mind arguing, Toby; it's all right, and I'm only joking. I get the idea; and now, has any one a scheme on tap that would apply to the case?"

Toby scratched his head as though he considered that, having been the first to make the suggestion, it was up to him to say something, no matter how.

"Well, there's the spring-gun trap, you know," he remarked, without once stuttering, which fact proved that he was deliberately taking his time about answering.

"What sort of arrangement do you call that, I'd like to know!" asked Steve.

"S-s-say, you a hunter, and never heard about the s-s-spring-gun trap?" exclaimed Toby, scornfully. "Well, I'll try to explain, if you give me a little t-t-time, and don't r-r-rush me too much. You see, a gun is f-f-fastened to the ground, and aiming along a certain avenue that the intended thief has just g-g-got to use in c-c-coming up to the b-b-bait. Then a c-c-cord is s-s-strung so the thief p-p-presses against the s-s-same, just like Max here fixes his c-c-camera nights, when he wants to s-s-snap off a skunk or a 'coon by flashlight. Well, the g-g-gun goes off, and f-f-fills Mister Thief with number twelve birdshot. When you hear the c-c-crash, and his howls, why, you just s-s-saunter out and f-f-fetch in the s-s-spoils. There, do you understand about the s-s-spring-gun trap now, Steve?"

"Oh! I knew all that before, only you mixed me up by giving it that name," the other hastily replied. "But it strikes me that'd be a pretty rough deal for us to play. It might answer if the thief were an animal, but a human being is different."

"All the same," retorted Toby, savagely, "he's a t-t-thief, and outside the p-p-pale of the law."

"Just so," Steve went on, and Max was surprised at his moderation, because, as a rule, Steve had always been the most reckless one of the crowd; "but suppose now we found that we'd done more than we calculated on, Toby? A charge of small birdshot starts out on its errand a whole lot like a bullet. It doesn't commence to scatter till it gets just so far away from the muzzle of the gun; depending on the size of the bore, and the way the barrel is choked. I've known a charge of shot to tear a hole right through a board when fired at close range. At a distance it would only have scattered out, and peppered the whole fence. And, Toby, we might feel rather bad if we found we'd killed a man, even if he was a thief!"

Toby did not answer to that fling. The truth of the matter was he shivered at the gruesome picture Steve's words drew before his mental vision; for Toby was not at all bloodthirsty.

Max now took a hand in the conversation.

"Listen, fellows," he went on to say, "it strikes me that when we set about discussing this matter, we ought to remember that there's one chap who's considerably more interested in the outcome than any of us can ever be."

"'Course you mean Obed when you say that, Max?" ventured Bandy-legs.

"He's the one," the other admitted. "And we ought to invite him to join us in figuring out our plans. Now, it may be Obed will have a scheme of his own that'd knock any we might think up all silly. I'll call him over, and tell him what we're trying to arrange."

It happened that just then Obed was passing on his way to the cabin. He had been working somewhere amidst his enclosures, perhaps making certain preparations for insuring the safety of his valuable furry pets, should a descent on the farm come about during the hours of darkness.

Obed hastened to join them. His questioning look influenced Max to explain without hesitation; and the woods boy smiled broadly when he heard how his new-found friends were already taking so decided an interest in his fortunes.

"Now, it might be," he started to say, again looking serious, "that all this fuss ain't worth the candle, and that nothin' 's going to happen; but I believe in shuttin' the door *before* the hoss is stolen; it's too late afterwards. I haven't got the time right now to tell yuh jest how I learned that my foxes was agoin' tuh be in danger; somebody I knew wrote me a letter, and warned me, which'll have tuh be enuff jest now tuh explain. Since I got that same, three days back, I've been figgerin' on how I could fix up a trap tuh ketch any two-legged varmint that chanced tuh come sneakin' around here of a night. Well, I got one er two tricks rigged up that might fill the bill."

"Of course you mean to show them to us, Obed?" Steve burst out with; "for if you didn't, and we were left in charge here, one of us might fall into the pit, and get knocked out, which would be tough luck, I'm thinking."

"Oh! I meant to show you, Steve," asserted the fur farmer, quickly. "And if so be yuh'll come along with me right now, we'll take a look at the contraptions, which, of course, yuh understand, are only meant for night-times, and tuh help out when Jerry wouldn't be around for me to sorter lean on."

Being boys who did things themselves, it was only natural that the four chums should feel a decided interest in what Obed had just said. Even Max showed an eagerness to go forth and examine the said traps. He could speculate as to what their character might turn out to be, but this only added a little more spice to the occasion.

So when Obed turned and started off, with a beckoning finger that enticed them to follow his lead, none of the quartette held back.

CHAPTER X

TRAPS FOB NIGHT PROWLERS

"Yuh see," remarked Obed, turning around as they drew near the first enclosure, where the parent foxes were confined behind the wire fencing, "I've just been adding a few finishing touches tuh this here trap scheme. I got a little idea while I was alookin' the ground over, and reckoned I could fix it up so there'd be a heap right good chance that a feller creeping around here o' a night would step into the contraption. I'll show yuh how I 'ranged it."

With that he led the way along a plain trail that seemed to be the easiest route up to the enclosure. Three times out of four a stranger, prowling around with meagre light to guide him, would be apt to follow that beaten track; and this was evidently what the shrewd Obed was counting on.

"Well, it's this way my little scheme is agoin' to work," he explained, after reaching a certain point. "See this rope—I throw it across a limb o' this tree. Yuh notice that it's got an easy runnin' slip-noose at the end, don't yuh? That I'm fixing right here, where there's a good chance the thief will put his foot in it as he takes this step I'm showing you."

He proved that he was right, and indeed it was really a difficult thing, after Obed had placed the noose just as he wanted it, close to the ground, and on little wooden crotches he had arranged there for the purpose, for any one to step across without getting his foot entangled in the rope.

"Well, let's reckon, then, he does get caught in the noose, and jerks it tight around his ankle," continued Obed, very much interested himself in what he was saying, and as Max quickly noticed, even neglecting to speak as he usually did, although he had shown this odd trait before. "What happens? I'll show you how it's going to work out, if everything runs as I've planned."

Accordingly, he picked up a heavy piece of wood that chanced to be lying close by, and which doubtless Obed had used before in order to test the accuracy of his figuring. This he inserted in the noose, and then gave it a hunch that not only tightened the rope but carried out the further purpose of the inventor.

Instantly things began to happen. The boys heard a queer rattling sound near by, and immediately the wooden "dummy" was jerked out of Obed's hands, to be drawn up until it struck against the limb of the tree fully ten feet above. Steve gave a whoop.

"My stars! but that worked like a charm, Obed, let me tell you. Greased lightning could hardly be quicker than the way you've arranged your trap. And what was all that rattling sound about? What's holding on to the other end of the rope, which pulled the log up on the run? I want to know, even if I ain't from Missouri."

The woods boy laughed as though quite pleased because his trap had worked well enough to call forth such words of praise from these new friends.

"Come over and see," he simply said.

They followed the line of rope, now taut, and resembling a huge "fiddle string," as Bandy-legs remarked, testing it as he passed along. It led them to the brow of an abrupt little descent, a sheer drop of perhaps twenty feet. Down this slope they followed the rope with their eyes and then discovered it was attached to a large and heavy barrel that could almost be called a hogshead, evidently something which had been used as a crate to convey a portion of the previous owner of the cabin's crockery ware thither when he moved up from town.

As the boys were no simpletons, they readily grasped the essential qualities of Obed's little scheme. It may have been original with him;

and then again possibly he had borrowed the same from some book he had read; but, nevertheless, it struck them as pretty clever.

Not content with the heaviness of the big barrel, he had placed a number of stones inside so as to add to the swiftness of its flight down that declivity, once it was released. The rope acted as "starter," and upon being jerked, as must be the case, should any one get a foot caught in the noose, it released a stake that kept the heavy barrel poised there at the top of the descent. The consequence was that it would plunge downward almost as though making a sheer drop; the noose tightening about the leg or legs of the unhappy wight who had sprung the trap, he would be jerked off his feet and hauled up, head downward, to dangle there in midair, as helpless as a babe.

"Set it again, and let me try the trick, please, Obed," pleaded Steve, who seemed to be particularly charmed with the arrangement.

"I will if yuh help me git the barrel back up the hill again," replied the other. "Workin' all by myself I've had tuh take the rocks out each time before I could push the old thing back again tuh the top, 'cause she's some heavy, believe me."

Steve, yes, and both Bandy-legs and Toby also, hastened to comply with this reasonable request; and between them all the heavy barrel was slowly pushed up again until the stake held it poised there on the top of the sharp declivity.

Max stood and watched operations, not that he was unwilling to lend a hand also if necessary; but just then he wanted to observe Obed, and draw certain conclusions in which he, Max, seemed to take considerable interest.

Then Steve was given the wooden "dummy" which had worked so like a charm, and instructed how to manage it, so that it would take the place of a man's lower extremities. Steve did so well that he, too, by a little jerk displaced the delicately arranged "trigger" as Obed called the stake, and caused the barrel to pitch furiously down the steep slope.

Steve had not been quite quick enough to snatch his hands away, after working the trick. The consequence was that when the billet of wood was plucked from his grasp with such swiftness, and drawn instantly aloft, Steve staggered, and might have fallen only that Obed clutched hold of him.

"Wow! did you see that?" gasped Steve, staring upwards at the dangling "dummy" as though he could easily imagine it a kicking, squirming human figure. "And say, it worked as fine as silk, didn't it? Obed, you've done yourself proud with this little game. If that thief ever gets a foot in your slip-noose his goose will be cooked, that's as plain as dirt."

He actually seemed to be very proud of the fact that he had acted as master of ceremonies, and set the trap off so successfully. Nothing would do but that Bandy-legs and Toby Jucklin in addition should be given the same distinction; so twice more was the barrel rolled up the slope, and on both occasions it worked to a charm.

"It seems to be next door to perfect, for a fact," asserted Max, upon being appealed to for his opinion; but he did not seem to "hanker" after trying it out on his own account.

Finally the weighted barrel was again pushed up to its appointed position and held there with the stake. When the proper time came, it would be easy for the inventor to arrange the slip-noose, and set the trap.

"What, is there anything more to be shown?" asked Steve, when Obed asked them to follow him a little further.

A few minutes later and they were gravely examining an odd arrangement which consisted for the most part of a very heavy log. Steve looked it over critically, and then ventured to give his opinion:

"Looks a whole lot like a deadfall trap, such as they use in most places to get bears in," he went on to say.

Obed chuckled as though pleased at the answer to his look of inquiry.

"Just what it is built on the pattern of, Steve, if yuh want to know it," he admitted. "The only difference is that in the regular deadfall the log comes down and smashes the poor bear by its sheer weight. Now, I've tried to rig *my* trap up so it'll simply make a prisoner o' the creeper. I'll show yuh just how it works. I've got a dummy here, too, that I use to test things. Yuh see there's always just a little chance it might go wrong; and I don't want to get caught, and made a prisoner, with nobody around to let me loose."

With that he demonstrated his idea. The trap was sprung just as he meant it should be, and if the dummy had really been a man, he would have found himself caught tightly in the log trap, with but a poor chance of ever getting out again, unless external assistance came along.

"Any more tricks like these two up your sleeve, Obed?" asked Steve, after they had further examined the deadfall, and Max had pronounced it skillfully constructed.

"Well, I'm afraid I reached the end o' my rope when I hatched up this second idea, Steve," the other remarked, in a sort of apologetic tone. "Of course I might think up a few more if I reckoned it'd be necessary. But I've got a hunch that one o' the lot is agoin' tuh grab that thief, providin' he does come around here. Besides, when yuh git right down to brass tacks, thar isn't as much danger o' my bein' robbed in the night-time, as in the day."

"And why not, Obed?" further asked Steve; "I'd think that was the very time you'd feel scariest, when it was dark, and you couldn't see if anybody was prowling around the farm."

"Stop an' think how foxes have holes in the ground, into which they c'n burrow when scared the least mite," explained Obed, readily, "and yuh'll see how hard it'd be for a stranger to lay hands on them. Now, in the daytime, if they came along, with me away from the place, a man with a rifle could knock over my pets as easy as turnin' his hand. But, all the same, I've fixed my traps. For one thing I'd like to find out jest who the thief is."

Max noticed what emphasis he put on that last remark. He could see the customary twinkle in Obed's eyes give way to a sterner look; as though he had brooded more or less over this same subject. And Max himself nodded his head as though he might in a measure understand just how Obed felt.

So they returned to the house. Bandy-legs at least rejoiced because with all those clever contraptions set, and waiting to give the intended thief a warm reception, it did seem as though there would be hardly any necessity for them to waste their precious time in sitting up and keeping watch, when they would be so much better off enjoying "balmy sleep," as he called it; and all sleep was along that order, according to the mind of Bandy-legs.

Max and Steve trailed along well in the rear. This may have simply happened, but Steve twice stopped the other, and pointed out something he wished Max to see; so possibly the delay was intentional on his part. At least, he presently made a remark that would make it seem so.

"It certainly looks as if Obed was a pretty ingenious maker of snares, that's sure, Max?" Steve was saying, significantly.

"That's right, he is, Steve, and we must give him great credit for it, even if his traps fail to catch a thief in the act."

"I was just thinking, Max," pursued the other, meditatively, "that it's evident this same Obed must have inherited that strain from a long line of trapper ancestors or progenitors; wouldn't you think so, too?"

Max looked at his companion queerly, and smiled as he made reply.

"You may be right, Steve, of course, but it strikes me Obed has an original streak of genius all his own, which doesn't have to depend

75

on any inherited trait. Things are not *always* what they seem in this world, you know."

"Lookey here, Max, you've struck a scent which you don't think best to share with your boon companions, that's as plain to me as two and two make four. You've come to think a little the same way as Bandy-legs, perhaps, and suspect Obed of being more than he lets on? Is that it, Max? Do you really believe he's playing some sly trick on us? Is that yarn about Mr. Coombs all moonshine? Does this fur farm belong to some company, that Obed is working for? I wish you'd tell me what you've got in your mind, Max."

"I expect to a little later on, Steve, never fear," he was assured. "I'm not more than half certain even now that it can be so, and I never like to make a mess of things. Besides, you know, it wouldn't be just fair to Obed to have us all suspecting him of playing tricks. Just go on as you've been doing. Take my word for it, this new friend we've made is all to the good, and will never turn out to be the wrong sort of fellow."

He started on after saying this, and Steve followed, looking very much puzzled, and shaking his head as though he could not catch the right idea. Shortly afterwards, however, Steve had apparently forgotten his newly awakened suspicions, for he was entering into the general conversation as heartily as ever. Still, Max noticed, with amusement, that from time to time Steve would follow Obed hungrily with his eyes, and on such occasions that double line of wrinkles, expressive of bewilderment, might again be seen upon the boy's forehead.

Toby and Bandy-legs were only too glad to take the preparation of supper into their hands completely. They felt a certain amount of pride in their culinary skill, and wished to show their host the full list of their accomplishments as camp cooks. Besides, they believed that among their abundant stores they carried a number of things which Obed failed to possess; and of course a new dish was apt to be a pleasant surprise to the woods boy.

The supper thus concocted and carried out was certainly a genuine triumph. Steve openly congratulated the two efficient cooks on their "masterly skill"; though Max laughingly warned the others to "beware of the Greeks bearing gifts," for there might be a base motive hiding behind all that glib praise. Steve protested that he meant every word of it; but then it was well known that Steve hated to do any cooking himself, and hence was fain to laud the efforts of others in that line, doubtless in the hope of encouraging them to "keep right on doing it."

After the bountiful meal had been enjoyed, and every one declared that it would be utterly impossible to eat another single bite, for fear of the consequences, they spent a very enjoyable evening alongside the fire that burned on the hearth, at one end of the cabin.

Obed, as he had promised, told them some of the strange things he had heard from the old sea captain, who, during his life on the Seven Seas, had met with many most remarkable adventures well worth repeating.

Obed addressed them in his own language, and Max often smiled as though some of the quaint expressions used by the young narrator amused him; though perhaps there may have been still another reason for his quiet chuckling. Steve caught him at it several times, and eyed the other in perplexity, as though he suspected Max of adding secretly to his fund of knowledge, which thus far he obstinately declined to share with his mates.

Later on, when they began to feel sleepy, Obed said he would go out and make sure his traps were set right. Max offered to keep him company, and together they sauntered forth, to be followed with a wistful look from the envious Steve, who was muttering to himself:

"I wish I knew what Max has got in that mind of his right now. I'm dead certain he's figuring out some sort of thing that's going to give the rest of us a big surprise, when he sees fit to spring it on us; but for the life of me I can't guess what it can be. Oh! shucks! what's the use of bothering any more about it? If it turns out worth while, Max will tell us in good time; and if he's on the wrong scent, why, he'll just drop the game, and no harm done."

After a while the others came in again, saying both traps were set, and there did not seem to be any need of their losing sleep on account of possible unwelcome visitors. Obed showed how the concealed bunks could be made ready, and, all of them were loud in their expressions of satisfaction over having such comfortable lodgings for the night. They mentally blessed the memory of the said Mr. Coombs, whose forethought and inventive ingenuity had planned all these wonderful adjuncts of the little forest lodge.

In due time they crept into their several berths just as if aboard ship; and after that several of the fellows did not know a single thing until they were rudely aroused, perhaps some hours later on. The last thing Steve remembered hearing as he rolled himself up in his blanket was the crackle of the fire, the mournful sighing of the wind through the tops of the whispering pines, and then the distant call of an owl to its mate.

He awoke with a suddenness that caused him to sit up, and consequently crack his head against the boards above his bunk. The blow almost knocked Steve back again as he had been before, and must have hurt considerably; but he ignored this fact just then, because from without there were coming loud yells of fright in a man's voice.

CHAPTER XI

A TREE THAT BORE STRANGE FRUIT

"Max—Obed, we've got something!" almost shrieked Steve, as he now tumbled out of his odd bunk very much after the fashion of a dislodged log, landing with a bump on the floor.

And Steve was not alone in his circus stunt, for several other fellows were making a hasty and undignified exit at the same time, Bandy-legs and Toby Jucklin, for instance. Max somehow managed to get on his feet without so much scrambling; and as for Obed, as he had been sleeping on the cot closer to the fire, they could already see him hastily pulling on some clothes.

"Get dressed, and in a hurry!" cried Max, suiting his actions to the words.

"Oh! listen to him whoop it up, will you?" exclaimed Bandy-legs, as those loud calls still smote the night air, and in a way that covered the whole gamut of human utterance.

Toby wanted to say something, too, but though his jaws worked, no audible sound came forth to explain the agitated state of his mind. They had luckily prepared for such a sudden call, and had their outer clothes handy, so that in an incredibly brief space of time all of the boys managed to get something on.

Then Steve snatched up his Marlin gun. Obed had already done the same with his rifle, so that when the latter flung wide the door and they trooped forth, they were in a condition to do battle if necessary, and at least strike terror into the heart of any skulking marauder.

Max, wise general that he was, had thought of something very essential to their success. This was nothing more or less than a lantern. They had been thoughtful enough to fetch one along, a clever little contraption that took only a small amount of room, and yet afforded considerable light. Besides, Obed possessed a lantern of the ordinary type, together with a plentiful supply of oil, looking to the long winter evenings when he might want to read in order to pass away some of the spare time, that promised to drag heavily on his hands.

So they poured forth. The cries still continued, and as vociferous as ever. Indeed, if anything, there was a wilder strain to them now, as though the fellow who gave utterance to the shouts might be getting sorely alarmed at his strange condition, and feared the worst.

There was no trouble about deciding which way to go. Even if they did not have Obed to serve as guide, and pilot the expedition, they could easily have followed the loud notes of alarm.

Everybody was more or less excited, from Obed down to Max himself, and small wonder when the fact of their being aroused in the dead of the night by this fierce racket is taken into consideration.

Hastening in this manner toward the spot where the first trap had been set, they speedily discovered that the overhanging tree bore strange fruit. Something grotesque was swinging violently back and forth. It was a human figure, but hardly recognizable as such, on account of the fact that it now hung head downward, with one leg firmly gripped by the tenacious slip-noose, and the other, together with a pair of wildly flung arms, cutting all sorts of eccentric circles through the air.

Never in all their varied experiences had Max and his three comrades looked on a more remarkable spectacle than the one by which they were now greeted. The man's face could not be plainly seen on account of his coat sagging down partly over his head, so they could not immediately tell what he looked like; but he certainly possessed a bull-like voice that, properly trained for opera use might have won him a fair amount of fame and money, for it was more than usually lusty.

He seemed to divine the fact that those in the cabin must have rushed out in answer to his shouts. Perhaps he detected the light they carried with them; or it might be Steve's loud cries caught his strained hearing at such times as his own breath temporarily failed him.

"Help me, somebody, why don't yuh? I'm strangling to death, I tell yuh. All the blood's running to my head! I'm seeing a million stars already, and I'll *die* if yuh don't cut me down. Hurry! hurry, please do, somebody!"

Obed looked to Max to say what ought to be done, for already he seemed to have come under the magical sway of the other's leadership.

"Take hold of him, and tie his hands behind his back before you think to let him down!" was the sensible advice given by Max.

Thereupon Obed instantly produced some heavy cord and started operations. While the boy deftly worked, the man continued to plead, trying to claw at him also; but Obed managed to get his job completed notwithstanding the interruptions. He was at the same time telling the unfortunate man to keep quiet, and he would be let down presently.

Steve stood by, gun in hand. He was casting uneasy looks around as though suspecting that if the fellow had companions near by, as seemed likely, and they should, recovering from, their alarm attempt his rescue, it might be his duty to stand them off one and collectively.

Bandy-legs and Toby sprang to where the man dangled. Max was already at the side of Obed.

"All ready, Obed?" he was heard to say.

"I've spliced his hands up in good style, Max," came the reply.

81

"Good enough. Now, Toby and Bandy-legs, take hold of him, and lift when I give you the word. I'll slip the rope off his ankle, and you turn him right side up. Now, go to it, both of you—yo-heave-o!"

It was quickly done, and the man, upon finding himself placed once more on his feet, staggered; indeed, he was so "groggy" after his recent strange experience at swimming in thin air, that only for the supporting arm of Max he would have fallen flat.

The latter allowed him to stagger backward until he leaned against the body of the tree under which the novel man-trap had been arranged. He was breathing hard, but seemed to be recovering from his panic; at least his cries had utterly ceased, which was one good thing.

So Max flashed the light into his face, while Obed leaned forward and eagerly stared hard at him. They saw rough lineaments, seamed and hardened by exposure to the elements; but of course the face was that of an utter stranger to Max. As for Obed, he was heard to give a *sigh* of disappointment, as though he too had failed to recognize any one whom he had reason to know.

The man by now seemed to have recovered in part. He was looking at the boys in a peculiar way; Max could not decide on the spur of the moment whether it was wonder or shrewdness that he saw there as the predominant trait of the man's features. But at any rate, since he had recovered his breath to some extent, he should be capable of speaking, and explaining how it came about he found himself in such a predicament.

"Well, who are you, anyway?" demanded Max, throwing as much sternness into his voice as he could. "Give an account of yourself, and tell us why you were creeping about here like a thief in the night?"

"What! me a thief?" shrilled the man, as though, again excited by the very idea of such a base accusation; "I never had that name, young feller. Them that knows Jake Storms say he's an honest man, if ever

82

there was one. I'm only a guide, and a trapper, but nobody ever yet caught me thievin' or poachin', I'd have yuh know."

"Where's your home, Jake Storms?" continued Max.

"If yuh mean whar do I hang out, it's this way," explained the other. "Last summer I was up at Paul Smith's place, workin' for the hotel. I heard some tall stories about the country around old Mount Tom, how full of fur animals it was, and so I made up my mind to spend the winter hereabouts. I built me a cabin away up on the other side of the mountain, and was agoin' to start settin' my traps when I got word that a gentleman wanted me to come down to Lathrop and git him. Yuh see, his doctor advised that he spend the winter in the mountains, and he thought of me, beca'se we'd been in the woods a heap of times in past years. So I was headin' for Lathrop by a trail I'd run across that took around the mountain, and meanin' to keep on as long as I could durin' the night, when all at once something flew up and hit me ker-slap! Say, I thought it was an earthquake, sure I did. And then I found myself hangin' upside down, with all the blood runnin' into my head. What's it mean, young fellers; I give yuh my word I don't get the hang o' it at all."

Max was not surprised to hear the man speak in this fashion. He had already made up his mind, after that one good look at the other's face, the prisoner of the barrel trap was a pretty "slick article," as Steve would have expressed it. And caught in the act, as he had been, it was to be expected that the fellow would have some kind of reasonable story to spin, in order to explain his presence there.

All the same, Max did not give the yarn the least credence. Something told him the other was deliberately lying, and the fluency with which he delivered that remarkable story announced the self-named Jake Storms an accomplished fakir, if ever there was one.

So Max, while not wishing to deliberately tell the man to his face that he was a prevaricator, set about catching him in a little trap. The others had also heard the explanation given, and were listening, with puzzled looks on their faces; at least Bandy-legs and Steve and Toby were, but Obed was shaking his head energetically, as though he put no faith in fairy tales; especially when coming from such unworthy lips.

"You said you were all alone, didn't you?" demanded Max.

"Why, yes, 'course I was," spluttered the other, uneasily eying the speaker, who was holding his light so that it shone directly on Jake's still flushed face.

"Then what did you shout so loud for, if you didn't expect any one to come to your assistance?" continued Max.

"Oh! say, yuh see, 'course I knowed thar was *somebody* around. I'd just discovered signs of a camp, and sniffed smoke. But before I had half a chance to make out what it meant, why something grabbed me by the leg, and threw me up like I was agoin' over the treetops. Who wouldn't a yelled, tell me? I own up I was rattled like everything. Anybody would be, wouldn't they? I couldn't understand it all; and right now I'm still agropin' in the dark. What struck me, and why does ye set such traps in the trail over on this side o' Mount Tom? Ain't the woods free for anybody to walk in? What have I ever done to any o' yuh to be treated like this, and have my head nigh jerked from my body. Tell me that, sonny?"

Max did not answer his question. While the explanation might seem to be fairly plausible, he felt positive the man was telling a downright lie; and Max believed he knew an easy way to prove it.

"Watch him, Obed, Steve!" he said to those who were alongside.

"Never fear about that, Max," snapped out Steve; "I've got him covered with my gun, and if he tries any slick game his name will be Dennis, and not Jake. Hear that, Mr. Fur Thief, do you? Well, mind how you tempt me to let fly with a charge of birdshot. I've got a quick temper, and a quicker finger in the bargain; so settle back where you are."

The man muttered between his set teeth. He was evidently feeling far from comfortable, because something told him these wideawake lads would not be so easily hoodwinked as he had fancied.

He was watching the movements of Max Hastings, who had dropped to his hands and knees, and seemed to be holding his little lantern so that the light would show him the nature of the ground. Truth to tell, Max and Obed, when last at the trap, had taken the pains to smooth the ground over, thus obliterating all previous footprints. This was done from a double object; it would conceal the fact that work had been carried on in that particular spot, in case sharp eyes were on the alert; and also gave a clear field for observation, as was happening just then.

Max quickly found what he was looking for.

"Come here, Obed," he remarked, quietly, and as the other eagerly bent over, Max went on to say: "You can see that here's another footprint, and quite different from the one made by his heavier boots. So he *did* have at least one companion along, perhaps two, for all we know. And that stamps his story a yarn made out of whole cloth. He came here, just as you expected, to rob you of your foxes. Killing them wouldn't have filled the bill so well, unless they made off with the pelts in the bargain. How about it, Obed?"

"Every word you say is true, Max," breathed the other, indignantly.

"Then we'll certainly not let him go free, that's a dead sure proposition," ventured Max, decidedly, and in a voice that he meant should reach the prisoner.

"Glad to hear you settle it that way, boys," remarked Steve, who had kept one eye on the prisoner and the other in the direction of his mates. "Shall I march him over to the cabin right away?"

Max gave a look around. He wondered where that other man could be just then, and whether he was watching them from some neighboring covert, having by degrees recovered from the near panic into which he had been thrown at the time his companion was snatched away from his side so mysteriously, amidst a tremendous din, caused by the shouts of the seized man, and the rattling of the stones inside the rolling barrel.

But he could see nothing. The little lantern only covered a certain amount of space with its meagre illumination, and much that was evil might lurk beyond the radius of its lighted circle.

"Yes, we'll change our base, and go back to the cabin," Max said aloud; "keep the guns ready for business, and if an attack is made shoot straight!"

Of course this admonition was delivered in a loud tone, mostly to warn the unseen party, who might be hovering near; but both gun-bearers gave evidence of meaning to profit by the advice.

CHAPTER XII

THE TAPS ON THE CABIN WALL

Once more they were inside the cabin. Obed was looking at the man again as though he believed the other was possessed of certain information which he hoped to obtain in turn. Max, too, was observing all these things with considerable interest, if the smile that appeared on his face from time to time signified anything. But he was studying Obed even more than he seemed to pay attention to the man they had found turned upside down in the tree.

"Well, one of your clever traps worked like a charm, Obed," Steve was saying, and doubtless meaning to compliment the fur farmer. "But now that they know we're on to their being around, it's hardly likely we'll catch another victim tonight. All the same something ought to be done to protect the fox pack."

"That's easily arranged," remarked Max, "we'll follow out the plan we talked over. Two had better stand guard at a time, and for several hours. They can be relieved by another couple, and in this way the balance of the night will be passed over. Those on duty are to carry the guns; and with orders to challenge any moving thing that comes along."

The man had made no resistance when ordered to fall in line and accompany his captors to the cabin under the pines. Once inside, he had glanced casually around, but Max noticed that he did not seem greatly interested. From this he guessed that perhaps the other may have seen the interior of the lodge before; Max remembered Obed telling them that some one had certainly been prowling about in his cabin at the time he was away, though evidently frightened off by his return before having a chance to do any damage.

"He isn't looking at these things, so strange to an ordinary cabin in the woods, for the first time," was what Max was telling himself; and consequently his heart hardened toward the fellow.

Having previously arranged all about signals that could be given in case of necessity, there was now little more to be said. Of course Steve had to be counted on as one of the pair to be first placed on duty; he would have been mortally offended had Max failed to honor him with this exhibition of trust. Then Bandy-legs offered to share his vigil, and Steve eagerly accepted the proposal.

"Take Obed's gun, Bandy-legs," said Max; "and remember what I told you about using it. Shoot low, so as to fill their legs full of lead, if you have to fire at all. And listen to our shouts as we join you, for we don't want a warm reception from our friends. Get that, both of you?"

Steve and his fellow sentry admitted that they understood what their directions were to be. Then they went out. The man had been intently watching all these things as though deeply interested. Since Max had found the second series of footprints, and thus proved the falsity of his claim of being alone, Jake Storms, so-called woods guide and trapper of fur-bearing animals, had relapsed into a sullen silence.

Of course he knew that the game for him was up, so far as attempting to deceive these wide-awake boys was concerned. Max wondered what thoughts were teeming through the brain of the man, as he sat there on the bench before the fire and listened to what passed between his captors. As for Obed, he cast many eager looks in the direction of the big fellow, and from the expression on his face Max believed he must be slowly making up his mind toward some move.

Therefore he was not much surprised to finally see the woods boy sit down alongside the man, who turned an inquiring face toward him. There was also a tightening of the muscles around his mouth, just as though he suspected he was about to be put to a severe test, and would have to gather his wits in order not to make a false move.

"Look here, Jake Storms, as you say your name is," commenced Obed, once more either forgetting to speak in his usual woods dialect, or not thinking it worth while to bother with it any longer, "I want to make you a proposition. Do you understand what a nice pickle you've got yourself into by prowling around my fur farm, and evidently trying to steal my silver black foxes? If we take you down to the nearest Adirondack town it means you'll likely enough, be sent up as a thief. How would you like that, tell me?"

"Huh! guess Jake Storms' got a reputation that'd kerry him through, all right, sonny," muttered the big man, but Max could see that he squirmed uneasily; likewise Obed must have guessed the truth also, as his next remarks proved.

"A reputation may be one way or the other, Jake Storms, if that is really your name, which I doubt very much. Perhaps some people might be glad to see you again. For one I don't believe for a single minute that you're a trapper, or that you ever worked for Paul Smith, who knows the kind of men he has around his hotel too well to hire a thief. I'm as sure as I draw breath that you came here to steal my blacks. Yes, and that you were *hired* to do this by another party. What was the sum of money he promised you, Jake, if you were successful; and is he around here with you?"

The man made no reply, though various expressive changes took place in the looks on his face. So Obed, after waiting several minutes to hear what the other might choose to say, went on.

"I said before that if we take you down to Lathrop you'll be locked up, and when court is in session placed on trial, charged with attempted robbery. Your picture will be taken, and sent broadcast to every city, so if you're wanted for anything big, the authorities will know just where to find you. That may not be pleasant for you to hear, Jake, but it's what I mean to have done. There's only one way you can escape it. Do you want to hear what that way is?"

"Yuh're away off the track, young feller," blurted the man, obstinately shaking his head in a contrary way, "I ain't done nawthin' to make me askeered o' the law officers. Jake Storms is my name, all right, too, and I'm meanin' to trap over on the Cranberry Creek section. And I'm on my way down to Lathrop right now to meet a Mr. Jasper, who'll vouch for my character, sure he will. But go ahead, and say what yuh meant to, boy. It won't do me any harm to hear it, I reckons."

"This is the chance you'll have to get scot free, and the only chance," said Obed solemnly. "Tell me who hired you to rob my fur farm, and not leave a single black in the burrows, and I'll let you go free. Will you take my offer, or risk a prison sentence, Jake?"

The man hesitated. That alone was enough to convince Max that he was guilty; for undoubtedly he must be weighing in the balance Obed's offer, with the possibility of making his escape through the assistance of companions.

"Ain't got nawthin' to say, boy," he finally growled, as though making up his mind. Obed started up, and hastening over to a desk at one end of the room he hurriedly searched through a drawer until he found what he was looking for; after which he again sat down beside the man with the tied hands.

It was a photograph which he held up before the prisoner, and Max could see it was a man's face on the card.

"Look at that, Jake Storms, and tell me, did *he* put it into your head to come up here and clean my enclosures out, so as to rob me of the work of nearly two years?"

The man started when he allowed his eyes to fall upon the face on the card; but recovering his nerve instantly, he laughed harshly and hurriedly snapped:

"I tell yuh, it's on the wrong track yuh are, boy." Why, I never set eyes on such a person as that thar. He's a utter stranger to me, and I don't know him from Adam. And I want to warn yuh that I'll turn around and have the law on yuh for playin' such a low-down trick on an honest man, just passin' along through the woods, and never thinkin' no harm to a single soul. I demands that yuh turn me loose to go my way. The woods are free as the air to everybody; that's the law. Further than that I ain't got nawthin' to say.

Obed was plainly chagrined, as Max could see. He evidently hoped to obtain some valuable information from this man; but it seemed Jake still clung to the hope that he might obtain his freedom without betraying secrets.

Max, taking advantage of Obed's absent-mindedness for a minute or so, managed to lean slightly forward and obtain a good look at the photograph. It was that of a young man, perhaps thirty years of age. Max was struck with the fact that the photograph certainly bore some little resemblance to Obed himself; and one could easily believe they must be related in some way; which, according to Obed's former recital of his widely flung family, would make the other a Grimes also.

The woods boy looked at the man several times, as though wondering whether it would pay to make any further offer as an inducement to the other to betray the confidence of his employer. But either Obed did not have the ready cash to offer a bribe, or else he deemed it not worth while, after the fellow had shown such a stubborn disposition; for presently he gave a sigh, and went back to return the photograph to the little desk, once doubtless Mr. Coombs' property.

Toby was nodding before the fire, and really paying very little attention to what was going on. In fact, he meant to crawl into his bunk shortly, so as to get a little more sleep before being called upon to take his turn outside as sentry. Toby not having had his suspicions concerning Obed aroused at any time, failed to take the same interest in the matter that Steve, for instance, would have done, had he been present.

"I hope yuh don't mean to make me set here on this bench all night with my hands tied behind me so cruel like?" remarked the man presently, applying his words directly toward Max, as though he, too, had long ago discovered how that energetic young chap seemed to be the "boss of the ranch."

"Why, no, we don't mean to be at all cruel," returned the other. "Here's an extra blanket you can have. I'll lay it out for you on the floor, and you can drop down just when you please. But don't expect that we're meaning to unfasten your wrists, Jake. We know a thing or two, and we're expecting to take you down to Lathrop tomorrow, to land you behind the bars. You've had your chance to squeal and get off scot-free; I doubt if another comes your way."

He did just as he said, spreading the blanket so the man could manage to roll over, and cover himself with its folds. This Jake presently accomplished. Max also noticed how he lay with his feet against the outer wall of the lodge and wondered at it, though without any clear idea that this had any positive significance. But time was to tell.

Toby had crept into his "cell," which was what Bandy-legs had dubbed the several bunks, built in the walls of the lodge so as to conserve room, and not be in the way during the daytime. Max, on his part, did not mean to follow suit. He thought it would hardly pay to try and snatch an hour's restless sleep when so much was going on around them. And, then, besides, he did not trust the prisoner wholly; believing it would be just as well to keep an eye on him.

Outside, all seemed as usual. It was long after midnight now, and if one listened carefully he could catch the customary noises of the woods at such a time, from the soft crooning of the breeze as it sighed through the pine tops, to the occasional note of some night-bird calling to its mate, or the plaintive voice of a hungry young coon waiting impatiently the return of its foraging mother.

Obed had thrown himself down on the cot, but Max knew he did not expect to lose himself in slumber. Several times he saw the woods boy raise his head and look in the direction of the sprawling figure of the man under the spare blanket. Obed was undoubtedly thinking still of ways whereby he might force a confession from the lips of the stubborn man; apparently he seemed to be intensely interested in discovering whether there was a power behind this raid on his enterprise. Max, remembering some things he had heard, began to believe he could see light in the darkness now; and from the way in which he chuckled to himself every little while, it might be judged that his thoughts were agreeable, on the whole.

Surely a whole hour and more must have passed since Steve and Bandy-legs started out to assume their duty as guards over the fox farm. Thus far nothing had been heard from the videttes, who were undoubtedly carrying out their orders to the best of their ability.

Max suddenly became aware that certain low sounds came to his ears. At first he thought some branch of a tree must be tapping the low eaves of the cabin being stirred to and fro by the breeze. As he listened further, however, it struck Max that there was a strange continuity about the sounds; they seemed to come in little fragments, with a brief hush between.

The boy was instantly reminded of certain experiences he himself had had in using a telegraph key while sending a message over the wires or listening to the sounder rattle off one from some distant point. Rude and uncouth though the dots and dashes were, Max quickly found that he could make out a positive word; and it was the significant one of "free!"

Gently he managed to turn his head in the direction of the spot where the man had lain down. He still seemed to be sprawled there under the blanket. A movement caught the eye of Max, and he saw Obed holding up a finger at him in mute warning. Thrilled by a sense of impending tragedy, perhaps, Max watched the woods boy slowly but constantly making toward him. Obed moved with the noiseless nature of a black snake creeping over the ground; his footfalls were so light that even a trained ear could not have detected them. He kept on toward Max until soon he had managed to reach the other's side.

Still those plain taps continued to sound in regular rotation, first coming from the outside, and then closer. Max believed the man on the floor was making use of his shoe to send a message calling for help; and that some unknown party outside was giving him words of hope.

But Obed had now gained his side, and meant to whisper something in his ear, so Max prepared to pay full attention. At the same time he glanced toward the door apprehensively, and was pleased to discover that, just as he believed had been the case, the bar was in position, so that entry could not be made by any enemy from without.

CHAPTER XIII

OBED LEARNS SOMETHING

"There's something brooding," Obed whispered the first thing; and then continued by saying: "What are those queer little taps, Max? I'm sure he has something to do with them."

"He's tapping the toe of his boot against the wall to send a message," explained the other. "They are using the telegraphic code. I read the one word 'free.' So, you see, there's some one outside the cabin, and they're hatching up a scheme to get him loose."

Obed grew very much excited. He looked toward the door as though inclined to immediately issue forth and investigate. Max thought the hope of capturing another prisoner was the lure that tempted him on.

"But what could have happened to Steve and Bandy-legs?" whispered the woods boy, as though suddenly remembering the pair supposed to be standing guard out there.

"Nothing has happened to them, depend on it," replied Max; "but this fellow must have been slippery enough to get by them, and reach the cabin, that's all."

"Oh! don't you think we might manage it, some way or other?" begged Obed.

Vague though his question may have been, Max had no difficulty whatever in understanding what he meant. His own thoughts were already ranging in the same quarter, and he could supply all the missing words. Obed was hoping that by suddenly issuing forth they might take the creeper by surprise, and effect his capture; such a possibility apparently gave the woods boy considerable pleasure even in the anticipation.

95

Max glanced again towards the door. They could creep noiselessly over in that direction while the man on the floor and his friend without continued their singular exchange of signals, remove the bar from its place, and opening the door dash out to take the stooping fellow by surprise.

But then three would be better than two in such an adventure. There was Toby Jucklin, a stout fellow, and usually well primed for anything that smacked of excitement and peril; he must be awakened, and enlisted in the game.

So Max held up a warning finger, and stooping low again whispered:

"I'll get Toby; wait by the door for us! Don't dream of going out until we join you!"

With that he silently slipped over to the opening in the wall occupied by the sleeping Toby Jucklin. The latter was easily aroused, and when Max whispered a word of caution in his ear, he knew enough not to cry out; though of course the blood must have started bounding like mad through his arteries.

Indeed, it was a most singular thing to be aroused from sound sleep by being told that danger hovered over their heads, and that it would be necessary for the three of them to sally forth so as to surprise the enemy at work.

Toby was game, however. His vocal cords might play tricks with him frequently, and give him heaps of trouble, but when it was a matter of action, Toby "took nobody's dust," as he often boasted.

Obed had meanwhile managed to creep over to the door, where he impatiently awaited the coming of the other two. The strange tapping sounds continued, and evidently the man lying there under the blanket had become so deeply interested in what he was trying to communicate or receive, that, so far, he had failed to discover there was any movement in the cabin.

Of course, all of the boys were quivering with half-suppressed excitement, though grimly determined to put their plan into operation. Obed had already reached up and taken hold of the bar, so as to be ready to remove it when joined by his companions.

"Keep the bar," whispered Max; "it will make a fine club, Obed!"

"Say when, Max," came back from the tightly compressed lips of the woods boy, whose eyes could be seen glittering eagerly in the firelight.

"Open up!" Max told him.

Perhaps the door may have made some creaking sound on being drawn back; either that, or else the man chanced to free his head from the muffling folds of the blanket just then, and discovered what was going on. He gave a shout of warning, and the three boys shot through the opening at the same instant.

Max led the way. He had carefully noted the location of the sounds, and judged that the interloper must be somewhere close to the wall where Jake Storms lay; so it was in that direction he leaped.

The stars wore shining brightly above. Besides this a certain amount of light managed to come through that small window of the lodge, and help to partially dispel the gloom without.

"There he is!" cried Obed, as they turned the corner, and discovered a figure in the act of scrambling erect.

Pell-mell the trio rushed at the unknown who just managed to gain a footing when he found himself furiously beset. There was a tremendous struggle. The man seemed savage at the thought of being caught, and struck furious blows. Toby at one time managed to cling to the other's back for a brief moment, but was dislodged by a clever fling that sent him crashing against a tree, and made him grunt like a hog that receives a jolt.

One thing certain, Max could easily see that the party they were attacking must be something of an athlete, from the way in which he fought. It is not easy to resist the assault of three enemies at once, since they may attack from as many directions, and confuse his defense; still the way this man struck out, dodged, tore himself free from their clinging hands, and conducted himself in general surprised Max very much indeed.

This kept up for almost two full minutes, with varying fortunes. Sometimes it appeared as though they were getting the upper hand of the unknown, and then by a furious effort he would break free again, only to be once more clutched.

In the midst of the fracas, loud shouts close at hand told that Steve and Bandy-legs, having heard the row, were rushing hurriedly to the spot, astonished beyond measure at the racket.

The man must have heard their cries, and the fact that his enemies were about to receive reinforcements seemed to give him the strength of desperation, for he suddenly tore himself free from Max, leaving his coat in the hands of the boy.

"Oh! he's gone!" gasped Obed, almost entirely out of breath because of his recent tremendous exertions.

For a fact, the man had vanished almost as though the ground had opened and swallowed him up. Even astute Max hardly knew which way to look for him. Then came the other pair rushing up, and demanding to know what all the row was about.

As soon as he could recover his breath, Max tried to explain. He had to repeat it twice, however, before Bandy-legs could grasp the astounding fact that some one had actually been carrying on a telegraphic conversation with their prisoner, tapping on the wall of the cabin to spell out the words.

"Say, you're stringing us, I expect, boys!" exploded the doubter; "it sounds just like a fairy story to me. But then there *was* some one here, because we glimpsed him disappearing like a falling star. I wanted to give him a shot, but I remembered what Max here said about shooting when in doubt; and we didn't just know but what it might be one of you."

"But, Max, he got away after all!" continued the disappointed Obed, as though to his mind that event overshadowed all others; "and I did want to find out if it was any one I knew. I believe it was, on my soul, for at college he always had the reputation of being an all-round athlete."

"Huh!" grunted Toby, rubbing his head ruefully as he came up, and limping in the bargain, "t-t-that was him, all r-r-right then, Obed. I don't know the f-f-fellow's n-n-name, but I've g-g-got his trade-mark on my c-c-cheek, every k-k-knuckle of his fist. Huh! he's an athlete, every time!"

"But don't tell me our prisoner skipped out!" cried Steve, in sore dismay.

"Not that we know of, unless he's gone since we dashed from the cabin," Max informed him. "And as we can't accomplish anything standing here, suppose we adjourn to the inside again. Toby will want a little soothing salve on his bruises; and I've got a sore hand myself, where I struck him harder than I meant to on the back of his head."

"It's too bad, too bad!" mourned Obed, following the others toward the open door. "Such a splendid chance may not come again; and I'd like to know, I certainly would."

When they entered the cabin, the first thing all of them did was to look eagerly to see if the man still lay there, Upon finding that he had not tried to escape during all the excitement, possibly being afraid he be fired on, they felt relieved.

"Anyhow, we've still got him safe and sound," declared Steve, exultantly.

"And he may make up his mind to tell yet," remarked Obed, picking up fresh hope, "when he finds that I mean all I said, and that he's on the road to prison."

The man glowered at them, though apparently he seemed fairly well pleased to find that they had not succeeded in capturing his ally. Max awaited developments. He was satisfied with the way things were going, and deep down in his heart believed the thrilling announcement he was storing up with which to startle his three chums would not now be long delayed.

"I s'pose we ought to go out again, and resume our watch," suggested Steve, after a short time had elapsed. "It's too soon for a change; and after all that excitement none of us feel a bit sleepy."

"As for me," ventured Bandy-legs, "I'm that wide awake I feel as if I never could go to sleep again while we're up here in the mountains, where such queer things keep on happening right along."

"S-s-say, I'm s-s-sorry for Obed," ventured Toby, who it seems had heard the lament of the woods boy, and could sympathize with him. "He had h-h-hoped to g-g-get a pointer by g-g-grabbing that streak of g-g-greased lightning; but after all, the fellow was too much for the whole b-b-bunch of us."

"But it's made me feel pretty sure now," said Obed brightening up perceptibly, "that I know who's to blame for all this trouble. I had a hint about it before, you remember I told you, boys; and while he kept his face hidden pretty much all the time he fought, I surely heard him say something that struck me as familiar. He wasn't a stranger, I'm certain of that."

"Well," said Max, quietly, "perhaps there may be a way to prove that."

"Please tell me how, Max!" pleaded Obed, eagerly.

"The mysterious stranger managed to get away," chuckled the other, "but he wasn't so clever about taking all his wardrobe along with him, you remember."

"Oh! his coat!" cried Obed, in thrilling accents.

"I hung on to that like a leech," now laughed Max. "Of course I should have been smart enough to keep my fingers on the man inside, but he had a slick way of just slipping out of the coat. First thing I knew he was gone, leaving me holding the bag, as they say. Want to take a look at that article, don't you, Obed? Sometimes men have a fashion of keeping letters and documents in their coat pockets; and between us I believe you'll find something like that here."

With these words, the speaker took up the coat he had torn from the back of the unknown, and tossed it carelessly toward Obed.

The woods boy snatched at the garment eagerly. Newly aroused hope could be seen upon his face. Everybody watched to see what the outcome might turn out to be. Steve and Bandy-legs, ready to withdraw from the circle, and resume their outside vigil, stayed their departure for a brief period in order to satisfy their curiosity. Even the so-called Jake Storms had his fishy eyes fixed on Obed, as though it mattered something to him whether the latter learned the answer to the conundrum, or was obliged to let it pass by unsolved.

So Obed upon receiving the coat, proceeded to ram an eager hand into the pockets, one after another. When he reached an inside one, he found a bonanza, just as Max had anticipated. There were some papers there, as well as a bill book. Bending down nearer the fire, so that he might the better see, Obed glued his eyes on his find. A few seconds passed. The fire crackled as it began to eat into the fresh fuel that had been tossed to the red embers upon the incoming of the party. Toby grunted once or twice, and continued to ruefully rub the side of his head, his right arm, one of his thighs, and, in fact, as much of his entire person as he could conveniently cover in a short space of time.

Then Obed was heard to give a low exclamation. His whole manner was a singular mixture of satisfaction and anger. Evidently, he had accomplished his set purpose, and the result had aroused conflicting emotions within his breast.

"Well, have you found out who the man is, Obed?" asked Steve, unable to curb his burning curiosity.

"Yes, there's no longer any question about it," returned the other, bitterly, "for here are letters addressed to him. I may even take the privilege of reading them tomorrow, for in that way I can perhaps discover some evidence that will force him to stop this ugly business. Oh! the meanness of Robert to strike this cowardly blow at me, his own cousin! He's a disgrace to the whole family."

"Pity the poor Grimeses!" exclaimed Max, looking straight at Obed, with such a queer expression on his face that presently the woods boy could not keep from bursting into a laugh.

"Max, you're on to me; I can see!" he cried, rushing up to the other and holding out his hand eagerly. "I've guessed for some time that you had your suspicions, and now I know it's so."

And Max, too, threw back his head to indulge in a good laugh; while Steve, Toby and Bandy-legs, with months agape, and eyes that were as round as saucers, simply gathered around' and stared at the two who were shaking hands.

"Hey! what's all this about, I want to know?" spluttered Steve; just as though he meant to say that no one had any business to have secrets from the rest; "looky here, Obed, since when did you forget that Grimes woods lingo you've been giving us right along! I'm beginning to smell a rat, that's what I am!"

CHAPTER XIV

A BIG SURPRISE

Evidently, Steve was commencing to get on the scent of the explanation of the mystery; but as for Toby and Bandy-legs, they found themselves up against a blank wall, for aught they could see.

Instead of trying to explain, Obed turned to Max, saying meekly:

"You tell them, please, Wax; it's only your due, after solving the puzzle as nearly as you have. I saw you turn back to that book again, and scan my initials in the front. That was why you asked me If Mr. Coombs' first name had been Robert, when it was not. But it's all right, and I'm satisfied I had my peek of fun out of it, let me tell you. Now introduce me to your chums, Max."

"With the greatest of pleasure," laughed the other, as he took hold of Obed, and waving in a ceremonious fashion with the other hand, he continued: "Friends, Toby and Bandy-legs, allow me to present some one to you whom you'll be delighted to know—*this is Roland Chase!*"

Bandy-legs stood as if riveted to the spot, staring, and holding his very breath through astonishment. Toby Jucklin wanted to express his amazement, and also his ecstatic delight, over the wonderful outcome of their mission; but alack and alas! as so often happened with Toby, while the spirit was willing the flesh was lamentably weak, and he could not make a sound except a sort of spluttering gasp, while his eyes blinked, and his face grew rosy red.

Still laughing, the so-called Grimes' boy proceeded to grip hands with his guests. He acted as though it might be a simon-pure introduction; as it certainly was, in one sense.

"I'm ashamed of the way I bamboozled you fine fellows, and that's the honest truth," he started to say. But on the impulse of the moment I thought of that Obed Grimes name; and once I gave it to you I had to follow up with the lingo. I guess I got balled up more than once, for Max soon discovered that I didn't always speak as a true Grimes should, and that gave him his clue. Yes, I'm the same Roland you started out to find, just to please my dear old aunt, bless her heart. I was planning to surprise them all by appearing in town with my five thousand dollars, after I'd sold the fox cubs, and then claiming my share of uncle's estate. I guess it's all getting plain enough to you now, eh, fellows?

Bandy-legs could speak at last.

"Why, it's as plain as the nose on my face, Obed—I beg pardon, Roland; and I can never forgive myself for being so easily taken in and done for. So you thought to invest your two thousand dollars in starting a silver-black fox farm, did you? Well, it was a daring venture, and I hardly think you would have made the game if you hadn't been lucky enough to meet up with that splendid Mr. Coombs."

"That's a certainty, Bandy-legs," admitted the other, who apparently was not at all given to boasting over his achievements; "yes, I was in great luck to be able to do Mr. Coombs a favor, and win him for a friend. See what he's done for me. But all the same, I invested my money in this business, and according to our partnership agreement, I am to have one-half the proceeds of any sales, so there can be no slip of the law, to beat me out of my inheritance; if only I can get those precious pups to the man who's engaged them."

"And this rascal you called Robert—is he the elder cousin who would profit by your failure to win out?' asked Max, although he already understood that this must be true."

The expressive face of their new friend clouded immediately.

"I'm sorry to say that it's so, Max," he admitted. "Those envelopes of the letters I found in his coat gave it away. The temptation was too great for Robert, who always showed considerable jealousy, because our uncle rather favored me. And so when he learned in some fashion, I'm sure I don't know how, that I was in a fair way of carrying out the provisions of uncle's will, he must have determined to try and spoil my plans."

"Oh! the cur!" snapped the indignant Steve, now seeing the depravity of the miserable plotter in full. "I'm glad that some of you managed to give him a few good licks before he broke away. And I'll regret it to the last day of my life that I didn't get a chance to show him."

"And b-b-believe me!" exclaimed Toby, with a violent effort, "he's going to carry the scratches I g-g-gave him on his f-f-face for a w-w-while. If I'd known that he was Roland's c-c-cousin I'd have dug a h-h-heap d-d-deeper, too!"

"I'm only hoping," Roland, as we must call him after this, since he dropped the Grimes family when he admitted his identity, said, "this will teach him a lesson, and that he'll leave me alone from now on. But Robert is a terribly persistent fellow, and I'm afraid his failure may only spur him on to trying again."

"Never mind, Roland," said Steve, dwelling almost affectionately on the name, now that he knew the one who claimed it, "we're going to stand back of you through thick and thin. If those fox pups don't eventually get to their prospective purchaser, we'll have to know the reason why. Isn't that so, fellows?"

"My sentiments exactly," said Max, promptly.

"Me, too!" exclaimed Toby.

"Ditto here!" added Bandy-legs.

"I want to say this," observed Roland with a suspicious moisture in his fine eyes, "it was the luckiest hour of my life when I ran across this bunch of royal good fellows. Why, only for you I'd as like as not have been *ruined*; because alone and single-handed I never could have stood out against two clever and unscrupulous schemers. And I'll never forget it as long as I draw breath."

"There'll be some people mighty sorry, though, I bet you," Bandy-legs hastened to add, as he looked roguishly at Roland; "by which I mean those poor Grimeses, who have lost tonight the brightest star in the whole big Grimes constellation. Why, I can just picture how they'll all mourn—Uncle Hiram, Uncle Silas, Uncle Nicodemus, and all those other uncles and aunts, with old Granddaddy Grimes weeping harder than any of the rest over the bereavement; for Obed is no longer in the flesh!"

The comical way in which Bandy-legs said this caused a general laugh; why, even the wondering prisoner on the floor, who, of course, could hardly understand the joke, had to grin at the humorous expression on the boy's face.

"Oh! I guess they'll be able to stand it, if I can," ventured Roland, "Please don't bear me any malice, fellows, for having my little joke. You see I used to be quite a hand for such things; but living all alone up here didn't give me much of an opportunity to try any pranks; and so I was just aching for a turn. It didn't do any harm, and afforded me some fun, so please forget it."

"But, Roland, none of that story you told us about your good friend, Mr. Coombs, was made up, of course?" asked Steve.

"That was every word of it true," came the quick answer. "Oh! he was the finest old gentleman you ever heard about. I grew very fond of him; and when I received word in a letter from his housekeeper that he had died, shortly after his wife went, it broke me all up. I moped around here for a whole week, and came near throwing the entire job up. Then I remembered how he had always put such confidence in everything I attempted; and so I just shut my teeth tighter together, and said I'd go through with it or know the reason why. And I have, for I'm on the point of success; if only that Robert doesn't upset the fat in the fire at the last hour."

"Well, he won't, you can just depend on that," said Bandy-legs, almost fiercely. "Here are four standbys who are booked to gather around, and see that you get the fox pups to market. Next time Robert comes where he isn't wanted, he may get a broken head, or something just as bad; for now we know his ugly game, we're not apt to be over particular how hard we hit."

All of which must have been very comforting to the boy who had taken such a big load upon his young shoulders, in the effort to show what he was made of. After all, perhaps the eccentric uncle who left such a strange provision in his will knew human nature better than most people do; for he had picked out the very thing calculated to spur a chap like Roland to do his best.

"Well," remarked Max, "since we've cast off the numerous Grimes tribe, and discovered the one we were in search of, and as the hour is getting fearfully late, suppose we postpone further talk until morning. There remain a few hours to be utilized in sleep. Steve, you and Bandy-legs haven't filled out your time as sentries yet; suppose you hold for another hour, and then turn it over to me."

"Just as you say, Max," replied the other. "I meant to propose that anyway, for the alarm broke out in the middle of our watch. Secretly, I'd like Mr. Robert to take his courage in both fists and sneak back this way, bent on further mischief. Do you ask me why! Well, I'd delight to make use of my scatter-gun, and let him have a mess of number ten shot at, say sixty yards. They'd pepper him good and plenty at that distance, without actually endangering his miserable life."

Max, knowing the energetic nature of the speaker, warned him against being too prompt at using his gun.

"Better go slow about that, Steve," he remarked. "Many a fellow has been shot by mistake. Every season dozens fall victims to hunters who see something moving, and blaze away recklessly. It might be one of us, for all you'd know. So don't think of firing without giving our signal."

Steve solemnly promised to remember. He knew the danger of handling firearms in a reckless fashion, and was not likely to offend. So presently, with Bandy-legs in tow, he went forth to resume their interrupted vigil.

Max and Roland sat there by the resurrected fire for a short time exchanging remarks. The prisoner lay on the floor and, as far as they could tell, seemed to have given up all hope of a rescue, for his heavy breathing was that of one whom sleep had overtaken.

Finally, Max pointed toward Toby, who could be seen lying on his back in his bunk, and evidently enjoying a fine time in dreamland.

"We'd do well to imitate his example, Roland," he remarked. "And as a last word I want to tell you again how delighted we all are over finding you; not only that, but discovering that you've been busy all these months. Your aunt is worrying her head off about you. The last words she said were: 'If only you do find, the boy, and he's made a mess of his attempt to win his inheritance, tell him Aunt Sarah has a place in her heart for him, and that if only he'll come back he can be her boy for keeps, because I find that I've grown to love him as my own.'"

Roland appeared to be deeply affected when he heard this, for he winked violently a good many times, and then, smiling, managed to say:

"You don't know how happy you make me when you tell that, Max; for she's a dear old soul, and I certainly do care for her a great deal. But it pleases me also to know I've made good, and that I can hold up my head when I show those trustees what I've done. The Chase family needn't blush just yet on account of Roland, though it ought to for Robert's mean actions."

So they, too, sought their beds, such as these were, and tried to forget all else in sweet sleep.

Max had a peculiar habit. Almost any boy can acquire it through much practice, and sometimes it comes in very handy. He was able to impress it upon his mind that he wanted to awaken at about a certain time. Once in a long while this might fail him; but nine times out of ten he could hit it in a most surprising manner. Many persons have proved this perfectly feasible; and although Max began it as an experiment of the control of mind over matter, it had long since passed that stage, and become a regular habit with him.

Accordingly, in just an hour after Steve and Bandy-legs had gone forth again, Max was out of his bunk, and arousing Toby, who got up rather loth to abandon his good bed and pleasant dreams. Still, he made no complaint, unless his frequent yawns could be counted as such, but trotted at the heels of Max when the other started forth.

The night remained calm. High overhead the gentle breeze still sighed among the pines, and whispered secrets as it passed through the fragrant green needles with their attendant cones.

Max took a single glance aloft at the star-studded heavens, and this told him pretty close on the hour; for in addition to many other ways of the forest nomad and believer in woodcraft, Max had mastered the positions of the planets, so that it was always possible for him to gauge the passage of time when the night granted him a survey of the constellations above.

When he and Bandy-legs had advanced a certain distance Max stopped and imitated the call of a screech-owl, so like the whinny of a horse. It ended up with a peculiar twist, and it was this that would tell any of the other fellows the sound was intended for a signal, and did not proceed from the real bird itself.

An answer quickly came. Then a couple of dim forms hove in sight, being Steve and his fellow vidette, ready to hand over the guns to their successors, and seek the shelter of the cabin for a little rest.

"Listen, Max," said Steve, while this exchange was taking place, "there's something queer out yonder aways; and I want you to try and make out what it can mean."

"How is that?" demanded the other.

"Why, every little while we thought we could hear a distant strange cry like somebody in pain. Of course it might come from a night-bird that we don't happen to be acquainted with; but it's been worrying us a heap. I'm afraid, though, the wind has shifted latterly, because we didn't seem to catch it so well."

Max hardly knew what to think of what Steve had told him; nevertheless, he promised the other he and Toby would listen for all they were worth, and see if they might have any better success in recognizing the strange sounds.

But the minutes drifted along, and at no time were they able to catch anything out of the common; so, finally, they decided that either it must have been a night-bird that had flown away, or else that change in the wind had kept the sounds from coming to their ears.

CHAPTER XV

STEVE'S DREAM COMES TRUE

"Did you hear anything, Max?"

That was the very first thing Steve asked on the following morning, when he poked his head out of his "hole in the wall" like a shrewd old tortoise looking around to learn if the coast were clear.

"We listened from time to time," explained Max, "but were never sure that we heard any strange sound. It seems that you must have been impressed with it considerably, Steve, to have it on your mind so?"

"I was, Max, and I am right now," admitted the other, frankly. "Listen to me, while the rest are busy getting breakfast ready over at the fire,", and his voice sank to a confidential whisper. "I had a dream. It wasn't so queer that it should come to me, after all that's happened. I dreamed that we came on that bad cousin of Roland's, Robert Chase. He'd fallen over a precipice, and was dying there on the rocks. Oh! it was horribly real, Max, and I woke up shivering. He was sorry, too, because he had been so wicked, and was asking Roland to please forgive him. And, Max, I've been wondering whether that dream mightn't have come to me to let us know we might do a good deed if we walked out that way this morning, you and me, saying nothing to the rest of the boys."

Max was struck by the thought that Steve must have had a pretty vivid dream to make him so tender-hearted. At the same time, he felt in accord with the sentiments so aptly expressed by the other.

"Steve, I'll go you there," he hastened to say. "It can do no harm, and may be a fine thing. Are you sure you know the direction fairly well?"

"Yes, because I was sharp enough to make a note of it last night, Max. You see, at the time the wind was coming in a lazy sort of way right out of the west. Later on it swung around to the northwest, which makes it so sharp this morning."

"Good for you, Steve," the other told him. "Then we'll head direct into the west, and cover the ground for, say a mile, coming back over another route. We can call out now and then, so if any one heard us they might answer. But you'd better hurry and get your duds on, because, unless I'm mistaken, Bandy-legs is meaning to sing out that breakfast's ready. And you know the last to the feast is penalized when the supply runs short."

"No danger of that happening when Bandy-legs has anything to do with the cooking," chuckled Steve, confidently; which remark proved how well those four chums knew one another's weak points.

Of course at breakfast most of the conversation had to do with Roland and his valiant attempt to "make good." He told his new friends many things that interested them exceedingly, and which were connected with his struggle. Their questions also brought them quite a fund of information concerning the habits of foxes, and how those who aim to raise the valuable animals for the great London fur market, go about the business.

"As for me," said Bandy-legs, who had been doing considerable thinking while all this talk went on, "I mean to try and hunt up a few of those bouncer frogs Roland here says inhabit his marsh. Of course I know that at this time of year they're deep down in the mud, and meaning to lie there till spring thaws 'em out; but it may be I can scare up just a mess. I'm awfully fond of frogs' legs, you may remember, boys."

They all wished him luck. Steve advised him to borrow a spade from the owner of the woods cabin, for he might have to dig deep. Bandy-legs, however, only grinned and showed no signs of a change of mind; for once he set his heart on a thing and he was apt to keep everlastingly at it until the realization, that it was quite hopeless, would compel him to throw up the sponge, which Bandy-legs always did with a bad grace.

So breakfast was finally finished, and the boys separated. True to his promise the would-be frog hunter set out valiantly on his errand, urged by his love for a dainty dish. Toby had agreed to assist Roland look after his fox brood, for there were many things he did not yet understand concerning their care, and which he earnestly wished to know.

This arrangement quite suited Steve and Max, for it left them free to saunter forth. They announced their intention of taking a little look around. Steve, of course, picked up his gun before starting, saying:

"You never know when you may want a shooting iron up in the woods. There might be an old wildcat prowling around these diggings, which would take a dislike to the shape of my face, so he'd attack us. And I'm homely enough as it is right now, without inviting a cat to make the map of Ireland over my phiz."

He and Max showed no signs of being in any unusual hurry as they left the cabin. They started directly toward the west; and once out of sight of those left behind, Steve quickened his pace a bit; at least he "chirked up" and began to show more animation.

"A mile, you said, Max, didn't you!" he asked.

"Why, yes, that ought to fully cover the distance," came the reply. "I shouldn't think you could have caught any ordinary sound even as far as that. Still, when the night is calm, it is wonderful how far even a groan will carry. The atmosphere seems to be in a peculiar condition at such times, and acts as a splendid medium for conveying sounds."

They looked to the right and to the left as they advanced. Nothing escaped the eyes of those two chums, accustomed to the "Great Outdoors" as they were, and having long ago graduated in a knowledge of woodcraft.

Some little time passed thus. They had so far seen and heard nothing calculated to impress them, though Steve was just as sure the sounds he caught on the preceding night must have been a human voice crying out in anguish. Doubtless that vivid dream was also making quite an impression on the mind of the boy; for Max found him unusually docile and thoughtful.

They had now gone considerably over half a mile. Max felt that if any discovery was going to be made, it must come very soon. He raised his voice occasionally, and gave a half shout; after which both of them would stand still and strain their hearing in hopes of catching some answering hail.

Squirrels barked at the intruders of their nut domain; blue jays screamed harshly as they flitted from limb to limb among adjacent trees; crows sent forth many noisy caws from atop of some neighboring pine, watching those moving figures suspiciously the while; and once a deer suddenly leaped across the trail, with a flip of its short tail, to speedily vanish amidst the colored foliage of some bushes.

This last event caused Steve to give a real yell, he was so startled. Hardly had he done this than he gripped the sleeve of his comrade.

"Did you hear that. Max? Was it an echo to my whoop; or did somebody really call out in a weak voice! Anyway, it seemed to come from right over there," and he pointed confidently as he spoke.

Max himself was of the same opinion, for he felt almost certain that a human voice had tried to attract their attention, though possibly the person giving utterance to the cry was so weak that he could not make much effort.

They changed their course a little, and headed directly toward the region whence Steve had pointed so positively. When Max held the other up presently and called again, all doubt was removed.

"Here, this way! I'm in pretty bad shape, I guess. Don't leave me, please, whoever you are. I'll pay you a hundred dollars to get me out of this scrape!"

Evidently, the speaker, whom Max decided must be Robert Chase, and no other, supposed the persons approaching, and whose voices he had heard, must be woods guides who might consider themselves fortunate indeed to earn such a royal sum so easily.

Two minutes afterwards and the boys found him. He must have fallen into the hole while hurrying through the forest, after breaking away from the grip of the boys at the cabin. He had been severely cut by a sharp flint-like rock, and lost considerable blood, which weakened him so that, as he afterwards confessed to them, he must have swooned away, and lain there for hours unaware of his perilous condition.

The two boys soon managed to get the young man up on level ground. As often happened, it was Max who conceived the easiest way of doing this. To lift a dead weight of a hundred and fifty pounds is no light task, and so he started to break away one side of the pit, thus raising the bottom of the interior until they were able to simply *carry* Robert out of the hole.

Steve was loud in his expressions of admiration.

"Whoever else would have thought up such a clever piece of business, Max, but you?" he went on to say, as they rested after their effort. "Why, if it'd been me in charge now, I reckon I'd have gone to all sorts of trouble rigging up some sort of block-and-tackle, so as to hoist him up; but you just knock down a part of the wall, and there you are, as neat as wax. Wherever did you learn that trick, I want to know, Max?"

"You'll laugh if I tell you," chuckled the other. "One day in reading about how some musty old professors are digging out all sorts of weighty treasures belonging to bygone days over in. Egypt, I chanced to learn how a certain Arab contracted to excavate a big stone weighing ever so many tons, and which the learned savant could not see how they were ever going to get out of the deep hole. Well, that Arab just kept filling up the hole, and lifting the stone inch by inch. When he finished there was no hole, but the great rock stood on level ground. And that, Steve, they say is old-time mechanical engineering, which has never been beaten in these modern days. The Pyramids were built in that simple way. Human lives and labor counted for little in those old times."

"All I can say is, Max, it takes you to apply whatever you read to working out your own problems. But however are we going to get this man back to the cabin! Must we build a litter and carry him?"

Robert seemed to be suffering from something more than physical anguish. A tortured mind can stab even more keenly than painful bodily wounds. Lying there and facing possible death, Robert Chase had evidently seen a great light. He beckoned to the boys to bend over him, and then in a weak voice went on to say:

"I don't know just how badly I'm hurt, young fellows, but I do know that I'm done with this miserable business. I've got just what I deserve, and it may be the best thing that ever happened to me. During the time I lay here and had my senses, I've made up my mind to ask my cousin Roland to forgive me, and let me make amends for the evil I've tried to do. I know now that it doesn't pay in the long run, for I've come near losing all my self-respect. Yes, get me to the camp, if you can. I want to face the music, and have it over with. Something seems to tell me that the boy isn't the one to hold a grudge against a chap who's been punished already for doing an evil deed."

That sort of talk pleased Max immensely. He saw that Robert Chase must have been having a terrible conflict between his better nature and the insatiate craving for wealth; and now that a wise Providence had stepped in to nip all his plots in the bud, why things began to look very bright all around.

It was found that with one of the boys on either side, Robert could manage to walk fairly well, although they often had to stop and let him rest.

It took them a full two hours to get back to the cabin, where their arrival created considerable excitement. At the moment, Roland was out somewhere attending to his pets, and so the injured man was made as comfortable as possible by Toby and Bandy-legs, the latter of whom had just come in carrying a pretty fair mess of frogs' legs all dressed for the frying-pan.

Then when Roland came along, to be told what had happened, and how his cousin was anxious to see him alone, he looked actually pleased at the queer turn affairs had taken. He went in and was with Robert for quite a long time. They must have had a good heart-to-heart talk, for when Roland appeared again, he was smiling broadly, and hastened to say:

"We've not only patched up a truce, boys, but made an enduring covenant. After this there's not going to be any war in the Chase family; and now that Robert has humbled himself to confess his wrong-doing, I believe we're going to be the best of friends. I've promised him, without his asking it, that I'll never tell a single soul about what happened up here. You must agree to the same thing, for my sake. I feel sure you'll all like Robert, when you get to know him."

"Who can tell," muttered Toby, as if to himself; "in time we might even g-g-get *familiar* with him. Stranger things than that have happened. I only hope he won't hold a g-g-grudge against me when he sees the mark of all my f-f-fingernails down his face."

"Just now, Toby, he isn't in a mood to bear anybody a grudge," Roland went on to say; "for he believes he didn't get half that he merited. But after all it's come out a thousand per cent better than I ever dreamed it would. And when I start off with my pair of grown cubs I needn't be afraid of any one waylaying me on the road."

"All the same," observed Steve, raising his heavy eyebrows suggestively, "we'll see to it that you have plenty of company on the way. Since the object of our trip up here into the heart of the Adirondacks has been fulfilled, I rather reckon we'll be wanting to go along with you, to see the fox pups handed over, and that lovely check received. Afterwards we can all start for Carson, where you and your good old aunt may have a family reunion all to yourselves; unless you see fit to invite Uncle Sephus, Uncle Nicodemus, Uncle Job, or some of those old worthies to join with you, so as to make things hum."

They all laughed at Steve's humorous remark.

"B-b-but what's to be d-d-done with this p-p-pretty thing?" demanded Toby, pointing as he spoke to their prisoner, who was sitting outside the door, having one of his ankles held fast with a trailing rope, so that he could not run away, even if tempted to do so; which, considering his helpless condition, with both hands tied behind his back, he was hardly in the humor to do.

CHAPTER XVI

THE FUR FARMER'S TRIUMPH—CONCLUSION

While all this talk was going on, the man had of course listened. What he had just heard Roland say about forgiving his scheming cousin must have encouraged the fellow more or less; for surely if they meant to let the chief conspirator go scot-free, it would hardly be fitting to take it out on the poor hired tool.

"I hope you include me in that general amnesty order, young fellows," he now hastened to say, with a wishful look on his face. "Since the fat is in the fire I'm ready to tell anything you want of me. Course my name isn't Jake Storms; though it isn't necessary for me to inform you what it might be, because that doesn't concern anybody around here. I needed money pretty badly, and the gent tempted me beyond my limit, so I agreed to help him steal the fox cubs. I was to have all they'd fetch when sold, and so I came along. But if you just cut these cords, and tell me to clear out, I'll vamose the ranch instanter."

Max nodded his head in the affirmative.

"You might as well make an early start," he remarked, drily. "Since things have turned out the way they have, we couldn't make any use of you. But before you go, understand one thing, my friend."

"What might that be, young fellow?" asked the other, though looking very much pleased at hearing he would be set free.

"Don't get it into your head that it's going to be an easy snap to come back here and rob this fox farm. You'd be a fool to try it for many reasons. In the first place, silver blacks are so few in number that any one selling a cub or a pelt can be tracked, and made to prove ownership. There's also an association forming that will insure these costly animals, and chase a thief across the continent until they eventually get him; just as the bankers' association does. Understand that?"

"Oh! don't bother about me," the man hastened to tell them. "I'm through with this sort of risky game. I can make a living at something that brings in easier returns; only set me free and I'll never come back here again, never, on your life."

"There'll be a guard here while we're gone," continued Max, sternly, "a man who can hit a silver quarter with his rifle as far as he can see it through the telescopic globe sight. It wouldn't be safe for prowlers to show up here. Besides, they could never find the foxes, hidden deep down in their burrows, during the night time. Steve, set him free, please."

The boys felt that they could afford to be magnanimous, since things had taken such a glorious turn in their favor. So they not only gave the so-called Jake Storms his liberty but filled his pockets with such food as would serve him until he came to a town. Roland was seen talking with him just before he left, and Max felt sure the boy must have thrust some money into the man's hand, for the fellow acted as though greatly confused, and shook his head while walking hastily away, as though the kindness of those boys quite overwhelmed, him.

Roland continued his work of making his cousin thoroughly ashamed of his recent mean actions. He waited on the injured man as though Robert had always been one of his best friends. If ever a fellow "heaped coals of fire on the head of his enemy," Roland Chase certainly did during the three days they continued to linger at the lodge under the pines.

Meanwhile, the signal had been set for Jerry Stocks to come over, and when he arrived, he turned out to be very much the kind of a man the boys expected to see, a homely specimen of a woodsman, honest as the day was long, and "filled to the brim," as Steve aptly expressed it, with an accurate knowledge of all such things as may prove of value to one who roams the wilderness.

He was to be left in charge during the absence of the young fur farmer. Roland had long ago won the sincere admiration of the rugged woodsman, who stood ready to do anything to show his regard. Besides, he would be well paid for all his trouble, and his family might even come over to visit him occasionally.

During the balance of their stay under the sheltering roof of the wonderful little lodge under the whispering pines, the boys made use of every hour in order to enjoy their limited holiday. Since success had crowned their efforts to find the missing one, they were in constant high spirits. It always produces a feeling of exultation to know that the goal has been attained for which a start was made; and the four chums were only human.

They certainly had a great time of it, visiting all sorts of strange nooks under the guidance of either Roland or Jerry. Max found a number of opportunities to add to his interesting collection of flashlight pictures. He made a specialty of the fox farm, and with the assistance of the young owner, managed to snap off the timid occupants of the enclosures in the act of feeding, as well as under various other equally instructive conditions; all of which would give a pretty good idea of how progressive fur farmers manage their outfit.

The wounded man grew better, so that when it was time for them to leave, he could take his part in the procession; though the others declined to let him burden himself with any of the duffle, since he was still weak.

Max had been studying Robert, and reached the conclusion that the young man was heartily ashamed of his miserable plotting. He hoped it would be a good lesson calculated to serve Robert the rest of his life; and if this turned out to be so, then that stumble of his, unfortunate as it may have seemed to him at the time, was the best thing that had ever happened to him.

The two marketable fox pups were placed securely in the cage that had been secured for this very purpose by Roland when last in the city. It weighed very little, and could be easily transported like an ordinary pack on the back. Roland himself meant to carry it, but of course the others insisted on "spelling" him from time to time.

Really, when the fateful morning hour came, and they turned back to give a last fond look at the little lodge under the green pines, Max and his three chums were conscious of a strange feeling of keen regret around the region of their hearts; which proved how the woods home of Roland had grown upon them.

"I certainly do hope those pictures will turn out to be daisies, Max." Steve was heard to say, most earnestly; "because I'll take a heap of satisfaction in recalling many of the pleasant things that have happened to us up here, where the breeze is always telling tales to the pinetops; and it's nice to be able to see what your mind is centered on."

"But look here," said Roland, delighted to hear Steve talk in that strain; "you mustn't think that even if I do succeed to that jolly little fortune left by my real uncle, and not one of the Grimeses, that I'm meaning to drop this fox farm business. By now it's got a deep hold on me, and I'm more bent than ever on making it a big success. Yes, and I'm also counting on you fellows paying me another visit some other time, the sooner the better."

They assured him it would please them beyond measure to contemplate spending part of their next summer vacation with him, when they could investigate still further the many delightful mysteries of the Adirondack wilderness.

So the lovely nook was lost sight of, and for some little time a silence seemed to fall upon all the members of the group, as they continued to trudge along the trail that eventually would fetch them to a road, and after that to a village.

Of course our story nears its end, now that we have seen Max and his chums accomplish the object of their search. They meant to continue along in the company of Roland, and see that the pair of beautiful glossy silver black fox pups were safely delivered to the purchaser, who intended to start a fur farm of his own in some other part of the country, possibly away up in the Canadian Northwest, and had taken a great fancy for the particular strain of animal Roland was propagating.

In due time they arrived at the city where this rich gentleman lived. He had, it appeared, seen and admired the fox pups while fishing in the neighborhood of the fur farm, and made a contract with Roland for the delivery of the pair at a certain time, binding the bargain with a cash payment.

It all turned out as planned, and when the boy received the balance of the stipulated amount in a handsome check he felt that he had a right to feel proud of his accomplishment.

Robert had long before then took his leave, and in doing so he squeezed the hand of his younger cousin, and assuring Roland that he meant to see more of him in the future. So far as Max could observe, the man appeared to have turned over a new leaf, and from that time forward was likely to show what was really in him besides his former desire to loaf and spend money.

And so in the fullness of time, the five boys turned up in Carson, where a certain good woman whom Roland claimed as his aunt was wonderfully well pleased to find his arms about her wrinkled neck, and his boyish kiss pressed upon her cheek. She assured Roland the first thing, that there was no need of his worrying about the future, because she had determined to make him her heir, regardless of whether he ever came into the money left under such exacting conditions by his deceased uncle.

Naturally, Roland was proud to tell his aunt that while he appreciated her fresh interest in his career, and would be only too glad to respond to her affection, at the same time she must know he had not made a failure, and that even now he was about to call upon the trustees of the will, to show them he had faithfully carried out all the provisions upon the fulfillment of which his legacy depended.

It all came out as planned; indeed, those same old trustees of the estate, living in another town, had the greatest surprise of their lives when that troop of boys called upon them, and the whole story was told; for of course Max and the other trio eagerly snapped at Roland's warm invitation to accompany him on this momentous occasion, so as to witness his crowning triumph, and add their testimony, if needed, as witnesses to the successful outcome of his plans.

Roland had taken pains to gather all necessary documents showing how he invested the greater part of his two thousand dollars, and how he was to draw half the proceeds on any sales. He also had the contract for the delivery of the first of the silver black fox pups, and after could, in addition, show the fat check covering that particular sale.

Everything had been looked after to a fraction. The old men found it difficult to believe what at first to their minds seemed so like a fairy story: but in the end they had to admit that Roland Chase had fully complied with every one of the conditions imposed on him in the strange will of his uncle; and as the time limit had not yet expired, he was fully entitled to his legacy, which in due time was paid over to him.

After that, Roland again departed for the wonderful "farm," where the most valuable crop ever heard of was being grown successfully. The other lads heard from him frequently during the winter months, and there was no discouraging report forthcoming. He now had Jerry with him constantly as his assistant, the guide having built a cabin near the farm, where he installed his family. It was nicer for Roland, too, since there were several children; and he could spend many an evening sociably, having taken up a phonograph with him, together with a fine supply of all sorts of records suitable for amusing a mixed company.

Max often allowed his thoughts to bridge the many miles that separated Carson from that lodge in the wilderness; and it required no magician's wand to enable him to see in his mind's eye the delightful surroundings that made the strange fur farm a possible El Dorado, where Fortune was liable to knock on the door and demand entrance.

It is with more or less regret that the writer finds he has reached the point where he must say goodbye; and he only does so with the understanding that just as soon as further stirring events worth narrating come to pass, it will be his pleasure, as well as duty, to place them between the covers of another book in this series.

THE END

THE OBLONG BOX.

Some years ago, I engaged passage from Charleston, S.C., to the city of New York, in the fine packet-ship Independence, Captain Hardy. We were to sail on the fifteenth of the month (June), weather permitting; and, on the fourteenth, I went on board to arrange some matters in my stateroom.

I found that we were to have a great many passengers, including a more than usual number of ladies. On the list were several of my acquaintances; and among other names, I was rejoiced to see that of Mr. Cornelius Wyatt, a young artist, for whom I entertained feelings of warm friendship. He had been with me a fellow-student at C---- University, where we were very much together. He had the ordinary temperament of genius, and was a compound of misanthropy, sensibility, and enthusiasm. To these qualities he united the warmest and truest heart which ever beat in a human bosom.

I observed that his name was carded upon three staterooms; and, upon again referring to the list of passengers, I found that he had engaged passage for himself, wife, and two sisters—his own. The staterooms were sufficiently roomy, and each had two berths, one above the other. These berths, to be sure, were so exceedingly narrow as to be insufficient for more than one person; still, I could not comprehend why there were three staterooms for these four persons. I was, just at this epoch, in one of those moody frames of mind which make a man abnormally inquisitive about trifles: and I confess, with shame, that I busied myself in a variety of ill-bred and preposterous conjectures about this matter of the supernumerary stateroom. It was no business of mine, to be sure; but with none the less pertinacity did I occupy myself in attempts to resolve the enigma. At last I I had not arrived at it before. "It is a servant, of course," I said; "what a fool I am, not sooner to have thought of so obvious a solution!" And then I again repaired to the list—but here I saw distinctly that no servant was to come with the party; although, in fact, it had been the original design to bring one—for the words "and servant" had been first written and then overscored. "Oh, extra baggage to be sure," I now said to myself—"something he wishes not to be put in the hold—something to be kept under his own eye—ah, I have it—a painting or so—and this is what he has been bargaining about with Ficolino, the Italian Jew." This idea satisfied me, and I dismissed my curiosity for the nonce.

Wyatt's two sisters I knew very well, and most amiable and clever girls they were. His wife he had newly married, and I had never yet seen her. He had often talked about her in my presence, however, and in his usual style of enthusiasm. He described her as of surpassing beauty, wit, and accomplishment. I was, therefore, quite anxious to make her acquaintance.

On the day in which I visited the ship (the fourteenth), Wyatt and a party were also to visit it—so the captain informed me—and I waited on board an hour longer than I had designed, in hope of being presented to the bride; but then an apology came. "Mr. W. was a little indisposed, and would decline coming on board until to-morrow, at the hour of sailing."

The morrow having arrived, I was going from my hotel to the wharf, when Captain Hardy met me and said that "owing circumstances" (a stupid but convenient phrase), "he rather thought the Independence would not sail for a day or two, and that when all was ready, he would send up and let me know." This I thought strange, for there was a stiff southerly breeze; but as "the circumstances" were not forthcoming, although I pumped for them with much perseverance, I had nothing to do but to return home and digest my impatience at leisure.

I did not receive the expected message from the captain for nearly a week. It came at length, however, and I immediately went on board. The ship was crowded with passengers, and everything was in the bustle attendant upon making sail. Wyatt's party arrived in about ten minutes after myself. There were the two sisters, the bride, and the artist—the latter in one of his customary fits of moody misanthropy. I was too well used to these, however, to pay them any special attention. He did not even introduce me to his wife, this courtesy devolving, per force, upon his sister Marian, a very sweet and intelligent girl, who, in a few hurried words, made us acquainted.

Mrs. Wyatt had been closely veiled; and when she raised her veil, in acknowledging my bow, I confess that I was very profoundly astonished. I should have been much more so, however, had not long experience advised me not to trust, with too implicit a reliance, the enthusiastic descriptions of my friend, the artist, when indulging in comments upon the loveliness of woman. When beauty was the theme, I well knew with what facility he soared into the regions of the purely ideal.

The truth is, I could not help regarding Mrs. Wyatt as a decidedly plain-looking woman. If not positively ugly, she was not, I think, very far from it. She was dressed, however, in exquisite taste—and then I had no doubt that she had captivated my friend's heart by the more enduring graces of the intellect and soul. She said very few words, and passed at once into her stateroom with Mr. W.

My old inquisitiveness now returned. There was no servant—that was a settled point. I looked, therefore, for the extra baggage. After some delay, a cart arrived at the wharf, with an oblong pine box, which was everything that seemed to be expected. Immediately upon its arrival we made sail, and in a short time were safely over the bar and standing out to sea.

The box in question was, as I say, oblong. It was about six feet in length by two and a half in breadth; I observed it attentively, and like to be precise. Now this shape was peculiar; and no sooner had I seen it, than I took credit to myself for the accuracy of my guessing. I had reached the conclusion, it will be remembered, that the extra baggage of my friend, the artist, would prove to be pictures, or at least a picture; for I knew he had been for several weeks in conference with Nicolino; and now here was a box which, from its shape, could possibly contain nothing in the world but a copy of Leonardo's "Last Supper;" and a copy of this very "Last Supper," done by Rubini the younger at Florence, I had known, for some time, to be in the possession of Nicolino. This point, therefore. I considered as sufficiently settled. I chuckled excessively when I thought of my acumen. It was the first time I ever known Wyatt to keep from me any of his artistical secrets; but here he evidently intended to steal a march upon me, and smuggle a fine picture to New York, under my very nose; expecting me to know nothing of the matter. I resolved to quiz him well, now and hereafter.

One thing, however, annoyed me not a little. The box did not go into the extra stateroom. It was deposited in Wyatt's own; and there, too, it remained, occupying nearly the whole of the floor—no doubt to the exceeding discomfort of the artist and his wife;—this the more especially as the tar or paint with which it was lettered in sprawling capitals, emitted a strong, disagreeable, and, to my fancy, a peculiarly disgusting odor. On the lid were painted the words— "Mrs. Adelaide Curtis, Albany, New York. Charge of Cornelius Wyatt, Esq. This side up. To be handled with care."

Now, I was aware that Mrs. Adelaide Curtis, of Albany, was the artist's wife's mother; but then I looked upon the whole address as a mystification, intended especially for myself. I made up my mind, of course, that the box and contents would never get farther north than the studio of my misanthropic friend, in Chambers Street, New York.

For the first three or four days we had fine weather, although the wind was dead ahead; having chopped round to the northward, immediately upon our losing sight of the coast. The passengers were, consequently, in high spirits, and disposed to be social. I must except, however, Wyatt and his sisters, who behaved stiffly, and, I could not help thinking, uncourteously to the rest of the party. Wyatt's conduct I did not so much regard. He was gloomy, even beyond his usual habit—in fact he was morose—but in him I was prepared for eccentricity. For the sisters, however, I could make no excuse. They secluded themselves in their staterooms during the greater part of the passage, and absolutely refused, although I repeatedly urged them, to hold communication with any person on board.

Mrs. Wyatt herself was far more agreeable. That is to say, she was chatty; and to be chatty is no slight recommendation at sea. She became excessively intimate with most of the ladies; and, to my profound astonishment, evinced no equivocal disposition to coquet with the men. She amused us all very much. I say "amused"—and scarcely know how to explain myself. The truth is, I soon found that Mrs. W. was far oftener laughed at than with. The gentlemen said little about her; but the ladies, in a little while, pronounced her a "good-hearted thing, rather indifferent-looking, totally uneducated, and decidedly vulgar." The great wonder was, how Wyatt had been entrapped into such a match. Wealth was the general solution—but this I knew to be no solution at all; for Wyatt had told me that she neither brought him a dollar nor had any expectations from any source whatever. "He had married," he said, "for love, and for love only; and his bride was far more than worthy of his love." When I thought of these expressions, on the part of my friend, I confess that I felt indescribably puzzled. Could it be possible that he was taking leave of his senses? What else could I think? He, so refined, so intellectual, so fastidious, with so exquisite a perception of the faulty, and so keen an appreciation of the beautiful! To be sure, the lady seemed especially fond of him—particularly so in his absence—when, she made herself ridiculous by frequent quotations of what had been said by her "beloved husband, Mr. Wyatt." The word "husband" seemed forever—to use one of her own delicate expressions—forever "on the tip of her tongue." In the meantime, it was observed by all on board, that he avoided her in the most pointed manner, and, for the most part, shut himself up alone in his state-room, where, in fact, he might have been said to live altogether, leaving his wife at full liberty to amuse herself as she thought best, in the public society of the main cabin.

My conclusion, from what I saw and heard, was, that the artist, by some unaccountable freak of fate, or perhaps in some fit of enthusiastic and fanciful passion, had been induced to unite himself with a person altogether beneath him, and that the natural result, entire and speedy disgust, had ensued. I pitied him from the bottom of my heart—but could not, for that reason, quite forgive his incommunicativeness in the matter of the "Last Supper." For this I resolved to have my revenge.

One day he came upon deck, and, taking his arm as had been my wont, I sauntered with him backward and forward. His gloom, however (which I considered quite natural under the circumstances), seemed entirely unabated. He said little, and that moodily, and with evident effort. I ventured a jest or two, and he made a sickening attempt at a smile. Poor fellow! as I thought of his wife, I wondered that he could have heart to put on even the semblance of mirth. At last I ventured a home-thrust. I determined to commence a series of covert insinuations, or inuendoes, about the oblong box—just to let him perceive, gradually that I was not altogether the butt, or victim, of his little bit of pleasant mystification. My first observation was by way of opening a masked battery. I said something about the "peculiar shape of that box;" and, as I spoke the words, I smiled knowingly, winked, and touched him gently with my fore-finger in the ribs.

The manner in which Wyatt received this harmless pleasantry convinced me, at once, that he was mad. At first he stared at me as if he found it impossible to comprehend the witticism of my remark; but as its point seemed slowly to make its way into his brain, his eyes, in the same proportion, seemed protruding from their sockets. Then he grew very red—then hideously pale—then, as if highly amused with what I had insinuated, he began a loud and boisterous laugh, which, to my astonishment, he kept up, with gradually increasing vigor, for ten minutes or more. In conclusion he fell flat and heavily upon the deck. When I ran to uplift him, to all appearance he was dead.

I called assistance, and, with much difficulty, we brought him to himself. Upon reviving he spoke incoherently for some time. At length we bled him and put him to bed. The next morning he was quite recovered, so far as regarded his mere bodily health. Of his mind I say nothing, of course. I avoided him during the rest of the passage, by advice of the captain, who seemed to coincide with me altogether in my views of his insanity, but cautioned me to say nothing on this head to any person on board.

Several circumstances occurred immediately after this fit of Wyatt's which contributed to heighten the curiosity with which I was already possessed. Among other things, this: I had been nervous—drank too much strong green tea, and slept ill at night—in fact, for two nights I could not be properly said to sleep at all. Now, my stateroom opened into the main cabin, or dining-room, as did those of all the single men on board. Wyatt's three rooms were in the after-cabin, which was separated from the main one by a slight sliding door, never locked even at night. As we were almost constantly on a wind, and the breeze was not a little stiff, the ship heeled to leeward very considerably; and whenever her starboard side was to leeward, the sliding door between the cabins slid open, and so remained, nobody taking the trouble to get up and shut it. But my berth was in such a position, that when my own stateroom door was open, as well as the sliding door in question (and my own door was always open on account of the heat), I could see into the after-cabin quite distinctly, and just at that portion of it, too, where were situated the staterooms of Mr. Wyatt. Well, during two nights (not consecutive) while I lay awake, I clearly saw Mrs. W., about eleven o'clock each night, steal cautiously from the stateroom of Mr. W., and enter the extra room, where she remained until daybreak, when she was called by her husband and went back. That they were virtually separated was clear. They had separate apartments—no doubt in contemplation of a more permanent divorce; and here, after all, I thought, was the mystery of the extra stateroom.

There was another circumstance, too, which interested me much. During the two wakeful nights in question, and immediately after the disappearance of Mrs. Wyatt into the extra stateroom, I was attracted by certain singular, cautious, subdued noises in that of her husband. After listening to them for some time, with thoughtful attention, I at length succeeded perfectly in translating their import. They were sounds occasioned by the artist in prying open the oblong box, by means of a chisel and mallet—the latter being muffled, or deadened, by some soft woollen or cotton substance in which its head was enveloped.

In this manner I fancied I could distinguish the precise moment when he fairly disengaged the lid—also, that I could determine when he removed it altogether, and when he deposited it upon the lower berth in his room; this latter point I knew, for example, by certain slight taps which the lid made in striking against the wooden edges of the berth, as he endeavored to lay it down very gently— there being no room for it on the floor. After this there was a dead stillness, and I heard nothing more, upon either occasion, until nearly daybreak; unless, perhaps, I may mention a low sobbing, or murmuring sound, so very much suppressed as to be nearly inaudible—if, indeed, the whole of this latter noise were not rather produced by my own imagination. I say it seemed to resemble sobbing or sighing—but, of course, it could not have been either. I rather think it was a ringing in my own ears. Mr. Wyatt, no doubt, according to custom, was merely giving the rein to one of his hobbies—indulging in one of his fits of artistic enthusiasm. He had opened his oblong box, in order to feast his eyes on the pictorial treasure within. There was nothing in this, however, to make him sob. I repeat therefore, that it must have been simply a freak of my own fancy, distempered by good Captain Hardy's green tea. Just before dawn, on each of the two nights of which I speak, I distinctly heard Mr. Wyatt replace the lid upon the oblong box, and force the nails into their old places, by means of the muffled mallet. Having done this, he issued from his stateroom, fully dressed, and proceeded to call Mrs. W. from hers.

We had been at sea seven days, and were now off Cape Hatteras, when there came a tremendously heavy blow from the southwest. We were, in a measure, prepared for it, however, as the weather had been holding out threats for some time. Everything was made snug, alow and aloft; and as the wind steadily freshened, we lay to, at length, under spanker and foretopsail, both double-reefed.

In this trim, we rode safely enough for forty-eight hours—the ship proving herself an excellent sea boat, in many respects, and shipping no water of any consequence. At the end of this period, however, the gale had freshened into a hurricane, and our after-sail split into ribbons, bringing us so much in the trough of the water that we shipped several prodigious seas, one immediately after the other. By this accident we lost three men overboard with the caboose, and nearly the whole of the larboard bulwarks. Scarcely had we recovered our senses, before the foretopsail went into shreds when we got up a storm stay-sail, and with this did pretty well for some hours, the ship heading the sea much more steadily than before.

The gale still held on, however, and we saw no signs of its abating. The rigging was found to be ill-fitted, and greatly strained; and on the third day of the blow, about five in the afternoon, our mizzen-mast, in a heavy lurch to windward, went by the board. For an hour or more, we tried in vain to get rid of it, on account of the prodigious rolling of the ship, and, before we had succeeded, the carpenter came aft and announced four feet water in the hold. To add to our dilemma, we found the pumps choked and nearly useless.

All was now confusion and despair—but an effort was made to lighten the ship by throwing overboard as much of her cargo as could be reached, and by cutting away the two masts that remained. This we at last accomplished—but we were still unable to do anything at the pumps; and, in the meantime, the leak gained on us very fast.

At sundown, the gale had sensibly diminished, in and, as the sea went down with it, we still entertained faint hopes of saving ourselves in the boats. At eight P.M. the clouds broke away to windward, and we had the advantage of a full moon—a piece of good fortune which served wonderfully to cheer our drooping spirits.

After incredible labor we succeeded, at length, in getting the long-boat over the side without material accident, and into this we crowded the whole of the crew and most of the passengers. This party made off immediately, and, after undergoing much suffering, finally arrived, in safety, at Ocracoke Inlet, on the third day after the wreck.

Fourteen passengers, with the Captain, remained on board, resolving to trust their fortunes to the jolly-boat at the stern. "We lowered it without difficulty, although it was only by a miracle that we prevented it from swamping as it touched the water. It contained, when afloat, the captain and his wife, Mr. Wyatt and party, a Mexican officer, wife, four children, and myself, with a negro valet."

We had no room, of course, for anything except a few positively necessary instruments, some provision, and the clothes upon our backs. No one had thought of even attempting to save anything more. What must have been the astonishment of all then, when, having proceeded a few fathoms from the ship, Mr. Wyatt stood up in the stern-sheets, and coolly demanded of Captain Hardy that the boat should be put back for the purpose of taking in his oblong box!

"Sit down, Mr. Wyatt," replied the Captain, somewhat sternly, "you will capsize us if you do not sit quite still. Our gunwale is almost in the water now."

"The box!" vociferated Mr. Wyatt, still standing—"the box, I say! Captain Hardy, you cannot, you will not refuse me. Its weight will be but a trifle—it is nothing—mere nothing. By the mother who bore you—for the love of Heaven—by your hope of salvation, I implore you to put back for the box!"

The Captain, for a moment, seemed touched by the earnest appeal of the artist, but he regained his stern composure, and merely said:

"Mr. Wyatt you are mad. I cannot listen to you. Sitdown, I say, or you will swamp the boat. Stay—hold him—seize him! he is about to spring overboard! There—I knew it—he is over!"

As the Captain said this, Mr. Wyatt, in fact, sprang from the boat, and, as we were yet in the lee of the wreck, succeeded, by almost superhuman exertion, in getting hold of a rope which hung from the fore-chains. In another moment he was on board, and rushing frantically down into the cabin.

In the meantime, we had been swept astern of the ship, and being quite out of her lee, were at the mercy of the tremendous sea which was still running. We made a determined effort to put back, but our little boat was like a feather in the breath of the tempest. We saw at a glance that the doom of the unfortunate artist was sealed.

As our distance from the wreck rapidly increased, the madman (for as such only could we regard him) was seen to emerge from the companion-way, up which, by dint of a strength that appeared gigantic, he dragged, bodily, the oblong box. While we gazed in the extremity of astonishment, he passed, rapidly, several turns of a three-inch rope, first around the box and then around his body. In another instant both body and box ware in the sea—disappearing suddenly, at once and forever.

We lingered awhile sadly upon our oars, with our eyes riveted upon the spot. At length we pulled away. The silence remained unbroken for an hour. Finally, I hazarded a remark.

"Did you observe, Captain, how suddenly they sank? Was not that an exceedingly singular thing? I confess that I entertained some feeble hope of his final deliverance, when I saw him lash himself to the box, and commit himself to the sea."

"They sank as a matter of course," replied the Captain, "and that like a shot. They will soon rise again, however—but not till the salt melts."

"The salt!" I ejaculated.

"Hush!" said the Captain, pointing to the wife and sisters of the deceased. "We must talk of these things at some more appropriate time."

We suffered much, and made a narrow escape; but fortune befriended us, as well as our mates in the long boat. We landed, in fine, more dead than alive, after four days of intense distress, upon the beach opposite Roanoke Island. We remained there a week, were not ill-treated by the wreckers, and at length obtained a passage to New York.

About a month after the loss of the Independence, I happened to meet Captain Hardy in Broadway. Our conversation turned, naturally, upon the disaster, and especially upon the sad fate of poor Wyatt. I thus learned the following particulars.

The artist had engaged passage for himself, wife, two sisters, and a servant. His wife was, indeed, as she had been represented, a most lovely and most accomplished woman. On the morning of the fourteenth of June (the day in which I first visited the ship), the lady suddenly sickened and died. The young husband was frantic with grief—but circumstances imperatively forbade the deferring his voyage to New York. It was necessary to take to her mother the corpse of his adored wife, and on the other hand, the universal prejudice which would prevent his doing so openly, was well known. Nine-tenths of the passengers would have abandoned the ship rather than take passage with the dead body.

In this dilemma, Captain Hardy arranged that the corpse, being first partially embalmed, and packed, with a large quantity of salt, in a box of suitable dimensions, should be conveyed on board as merchandise. Nothing was to be said of the lady's decease; and, as it was well understood that Mr. Wyatt had engaged passage for his wife, it became necessary that some person should personate her during the voyage. This the deceased's lady's maid was easily prevailed on to do. The extra state-room, originally engaged for this girl during her mistress' life, was now merely retained. In this state-room the pseudo-wife slept, of course, every night. In the daytime she performed, to the best of her ability, the part of her mistress— whose person, it had been carefully ascertained, was unknown to any of the passengers on board.

My own mistakes arose, naturally enough, through too careless, too inquisitive, and too impulsive a temperament. But of late, it is a rare thing that I sleep soundly at night. There is a countenance which haunts me, turn as I will. There is an hysterical laugh which will forever ring within my ears.

LaVergne, TN USA
29 May 2010
184436LV00001B/64/P